TRAVIS McGEE

An astute and outspoken commentator on 20th-century life . . . a man of intelligence, wit, and compassion . . . a modern-day philosopher whose observations chronicle a changing world. With each book, McGee gets older, wiser, and more cynical . . . but always better at adapting himself to a world he both renounces and respects.

"MacDONALD'S BOOKS ARE NARCOTIC AND, ONCE HOOKED, A READER CAN'T KICK THE HABIT UNTIL THE SUPPLY RUNS OUT." *Chicago Tribune Book World*

"The author of the justly famous Travis McGee series . . . knows everything dangerous there is to know about people . . . in a John D. MacDonald novel, you learn how a lot of things work . . . Some of the lessons are not at all good for you, but they are as fascinating as staring at a cobra."
The New York Times

"One of MacDonald's most admirable qualities as a novelist is that he almost unfailingly manages to deliver precisely the pleasures that his readers anticipate . . . he has much to say, all of it interesting . . . believable and occasionally breathtaking." *The Washington Post Book World*

"TRAVIS McGEE IS ONE OF THE MOST ENDURING AND UNUSUAL HEROES IN DETECTIVE FICTION." *The Baltimore Sun*

Get to know one of fiction's most enduring heroes by reading the twenty Travis McGee novels in order . . . right up to his latest smash best seller, *Cinnamon Skin.*

THE DEEP BLUE GOOD-BY

NIGHTMARE IN PINK

A PURPLE PLACE FOR DYING

THE QUICK RED FOX

A DEADLY SHADE OF GOLD

BRIGHT ORANGE FOR THE SHROUD

DARKER THAN AMBER

ONE FEARFUL YELLOW EYE

PALE GRAY FOR GUILT

THE GIRL IN THE PLAIN BROWN WRAPPER

DRESS HER IN INDIGO

THE LONG LAVENDER LOOK

A TAN AND SANDY SILENCE

THE SCARLET RUSE

THE TURQUOISE LAMENT

THE DREADFUL LEMON SKY

THE EMPTY COPPER SEA

THE GREEN RIPPER

FREE FALL IN CRIMSON

CINNAMON SKIN

John D. MacDonald

NIGHTMARE
IN
PINK

FAWCETT GOLD MEDAL • NEW YORK

A Fawcett Gold Medal Book

Published by Ballantine Books

Copyright © 1964 by John MacDonald Publishing, Inc.

ISBN 0-449-12985-3

Manufactured in the United States of America

First Fawcett Gold Medal Edition: May 1964
First Ballantine Books Edition: January 1983
Fourth Printing: February 1985

one

SHE WORKED in one of those Park Avenue buildings which tourists feel obligated to photograph. It's a nice building to visit, but they wouldn't want to live there.

She worked on the twentieth floor, for one of those self-important little companies which design packages for things. I arrived at five, as arranged, and sent my name in, and she came out into the little reception area, wearing a smock to prove that she did her stint at the old drawing board.

Nina Gibson. She was a bouffante little girl. I had seen a picture of her at age twelve. At twice that, she had changed. Mike had carried her picture in his wallet. Now she had a pile of blue-black curls, Mike's blue blue eyes, small defiant face, skin like cream. She had one of those hearty little figures typical of a certain type of small girl. The hand-span waist, and the rich solid swell of goodies above and below.

"You'll have to wait a little while," she said. "I'm sorry."

"Then when you come out the next time you smile and say hello."

"Should I? This isn't my idea, Mr. McGee."

"It's called a social amenity, Nina."

"There won't be many of those," she said, and went back into the mystic depths of her profession. I sat amid the cased displays of household words. Three cents worth of squeeze bottles, plus two cents worth of homogenized goo, plus prime-time television equals 28 million annual sales at 69¢ each. This is the heartbeat of industrial America. I sat and watched the receptionist. She was used to being watched, but she liked it. She was packaged too. One (1) receptionist, nubile, w/English accent, indefinitely tweedy, veddy country. The little company was up to date. They had one that looked as if she were sitting in a spring wind blowing off the moors, with her steed tethered in the hall.

Nina came out—gloved, pursed, be-hatted, wearing a fall

suit a little too tailored for her structure—came out with a frail and indefinite-looking man and paused to argue with him, saying, "Freddie, if you show him three, he'll bog, and you know it, dear. That little mind can make a choice of the best of two, if the choice is obvious. So make the presentation of just Tommy's and Mary Jane's. They're the best and the worst so far, and he'll pick Tommy's and we're in."

Freddie shrugged and sighed and went back in. Nina nodded imperiously at me and we went out and rode down in the musical elevator and walked a block and a half to a lounge in a muted little hotel where the prism spots gleamed down on an expensive assortment of coiffing and barbering, furs and tailored shoulders, sparkling glassware, lovely people maneuvering each other into his or that unspeakable thing by means of quiet smiles and quiet talk and deadly martinis. We found a banquette against a quiet wall, and she ungloved herself, leaned to the offered light, ordered a dry sherry.

She stared at me, mocking and defensive. "The fabulous Travis McGee. Fabulous means something about fables. I don't need any fables. Thank you so much."

"From a very old picture, I didn't think you'd be this pretty."

"I'm a darling girl."

I didn't want to be within fifteen hundred miles of this darling girl. I didn't want to be in this October city. I wanted to be back aboard my Busted Flush moored in Slip F-18, Bahia Mar, Lauderdale, my 52 feet of custom houseboat which I could fill with my favorite brand of darling girls, the brown untroubled ones, eager galley slaves, the hair-salty, rump-sandy, beer-opening, fish-catching, happy-making girls in sun-faded fabrics, sun-streaked hair. But Miss Nina looked at me out of her brother Mike's true blue eyes, and he had never asked me for anything else.

"I'll tell you a story," I said.

"Oh please do, sir," she said.

"There was a little matter of a thirty-six hour pass, and our captain did not think he could spare us both. So Mike and I had some small games and wagers and I won, jeeped back, flew out, spent all those Japanese hours in a silk robe and in deep hot steaming water and on a pallet on a polished floor in a paper room with a darling girl whose name I couldn't say, and I called her Missy. She scrubbed me and fed me and loved me. She was five feet tall and giggled into her hands. And what made all the pleasure the sweeter was thinking of poor Mike stuck back there. So I flew back and jeeped back and they said he was dead. Either he had died at the aid station, or at the station hospital, or en route to the general hospital. Nobody was sure. Then they said he was still alive, but would die. And now, of course, he is, like they say, the ward of a grateful republic, and he can't see and he can't walk, and it is a gala day when they wheel him into the sunshine for an hour, but through all those miracles of medical science, they kept Mike Gibson alive. The point of the story is guilt, Miss Nina. Guilt because I am glad it was Mike instead of remarkable, valuable old me. I don't want to be glad, but I am. Then there's another kind of guilt. I've visited him about once a year, on the average. Do I go to see him to prove to myself it happened to him instead of to me? Should I see him oftener, or not at all? I don't know. I do know one thing. The nurse wrote me he wanted to see me. I went there. He told me about your visit. He said find out. So, with your help or without it, Miss Nina, I find out."

"How terribly dear!" she said. "How ineffably buddy-buddy! I shouldn't have gone running to him with my little heartache, Mr. McGee. It was selfish of me. It upset him, and it didn't do me any particular good. How can he check up on anything anyway? Why don't you just invent some soothing little story for him and go down and tell it to him and then go back to your beach-bum career, whatever it is?"

"Because he may be all chopped up, but he's not stupid."

"It's too late now. Meddling won't do any good."

"Maybe there's some questions you both want answered."

For just a moment the vulnerability showed in her mouth and in her voice. "Answers? What good are answers? The boy is dead."

"I can poke around a little."

"You? Really now, Mr. McGee. You are spectacularly huge, and a tan that deep is almost vulgar, and you have a kind of leathery fading boyish charm, but this is not and never was a game for dilettantes, for jolly boys, for the favor-for-an-old-buddy routine. No gray-eyed wonder with a big white grin can solve anything or retrieve anything by blundering around in my life. Thanks for the gesture. But this isn't television. I don't need a big brother. So why don't you just go on back to your fun and games?"

"I will, when I'm ready."

"My fiancé is dead. Howard Plummer is dead." She glowered at me and banged the table with a small fist. "He's in the ground, dead. And he wasn't what I thought he was. And

7

I'm trying to get over it, to get over losing him and to get over being a fool. So please don't stir it all ..."

"What did you do with the money?"

It stopped her. She stared at me. "What money?"

"The money you started to tell Mike about."

"But I didn't tell him. I stopped myself."

"Nina, it was as good as telling him. He lies there and hears all the words you don't quite say. That's why I can't go back to him with a soothing story. What about the money?"

"It's nothing to do with you."

"It has now."

"Please don't try to be earnest and domineering, Mr. Mc-Gee. I am not going to lean on you."

"I've come blundering into your life, Nina, at Mike's request. Plummer was killed in August. The police investigated it. I can come stumbling onto the scene and tell them that Plummer had a good piece of cash tucked away and his girl friend has it now, and suggest that maybe there was some connection."

"You wouldn't *do* that!"

"Why not?"

"There wasn't any connection. That's stupid. It would just get me into a lot of trouble. My God, my brother asked you to come here to help me, not get me into a mess. I don't want any help."

"Miss Nina," I said, smiling my very best disarming smile, "let's get straightened away. Being a beach bum takes money. If you want to do it with flair. If the money comes in regularly, then you're working for it, and you lose your status. I have to come by it in chunks now and then, to protect my way of life. Now I don't really think I would have had much creative interest in the life and times of Nina Gibson if you hadn't given your brother the impression your boyfriend had been clipping a pretty good piece of money somehow. When I heard that, my ears lifted into little tufted points. Where there was some, there might be more. I like to ride to the rescue when I think that's where the money is."

She had herself a startled and agonizing reappraisal. With trembling hand she tried to sip from a glass already empty. I caught a suave passing eye and signaled another round.

"What are you anyway?" she whispered.

"Your friend and protector, Nina."

She tried to laugh. "This is really ironic, isn't it? Poor Mike, trying to take care of little sister, and he sicks a big bland monster on me."

"We're going to have a lot of nice talks, little sister."

She narrowed those very blue eyes. The lashes were very black, very dense, very long. "I don't want any nice talks. I know I was stupid about the money. I haven't touched it. I haven't told anybody about it. I almost told Mike, but that is as close as I've come to telling anyone." She glanced at our banquette neighbors and lowered her voice, leaned slightly toward me. "McGee, if I had thought for one moment there was any connection between Howie's death and that money, I would have told the police myself. And all the time he was giving me that righteous conversation about his honesty and his responsibility, he was stealing from Mr. Armister just like the rest of them. Finding that money just about broke my heart forever, McGee. I don't *want* it. I don't want that kind of money. I've thought of burning it. You can solve my little problem. I'll *give* it to you. You can take it and go away. It's quite a lot of money. Exactly ten thousand dollars."

"What makes you think he stole it?"

"Don't you think I've tried to think of every other possible way he could have gotten it? I was going to *marry* him. I *loved* him. I thought we knew everything about each other. I thought he was acting so strange because he was so worried about what they were doing to Mr. Armister. But after I found the money, I knew why he was acting strange. I'll *give* it to you, Mr. McGee. And you can go away and leave me alone."

Her control broke. Tears clotted the lashes. She rummaged her purse, found tissue and honked into it. She gave me a despairing glance and went trotting off to the ladies' room.

I sipped my new drink and remembered Mike's troubled voice in the afternoon quiet of the wing of the veterans hospital in North Carolina. "The thing is, Trav," he had said, "Nina was always loved. Maybe that's a bad thing. It gives people that terrible confidence that the world is going to give them the chance to fulfill themselves. Plummer sounded like the right kind of a man. She opened her heart to him, all the way. The people who have always been loved have that awful capacity for giving. Now that he's dead, she can't forgive him. It's souring her. Trav, I can pay all expenses if you . . ."

"Expenses, hell."

"Was he a bum? Nina has always seen things as black or white. She's always been honest with herself. If you could just find out about that guy. Then make her understand why

9

he did whatever he did. Otherwise I think she's going to destroy . . . that special something she's always had."

"She won't want me meddling around."

"Shake her up if you have to, Trav. The way she was when she came here, it bothers me. That's not Nina. All that bitterness. She's trying to hate herself. Maybe because she thinks she was a fool about Plummer."

"The very nicest girls get taken by the worst types, Mike."

"If that's the way it was, find out for sure. And see what you can do to help her get over it. But don't take too much time over it."

I hadn't liked the sound of that. But when I questioned him he said that he merely meant he didn't want to ask me to waste too much of my time on this kind of a personal favor. After I left him I had a few minutes with the nurse who had cared for him for several years—a muscular and colorless little woman. She looked up at me and her eyes slowly filled at my question, but she did not look away. She nodded her head abruptly. "They want to operate again. He asked them if they could hold off for awhile."

"What are the odds?"

"Without it he won't last much longer. Maybe even if it's successful, he won't last long. But he's fooled everybody for a long time. Mike is a wonderful man. We all go to him with our troubles—even some of the doctors. And there's nothing we can ever do for him. I envy you, Mr. McGee, being able to do something for him. They say he used to be bitter. But that was before my time. I love him. I have a husband I love too. Do you know what I'm trying to say?"

"I think so."

"When he's gone, I can't stay here. I couldn't."

"He's fooled everybody many times, Nurse."

She bobbed her head and turned and walked swiftly away, walking with her shoulders high as though hunched against an anticipated blow.

So here I was, shaking up little sister. The one so well-loved. She had slammed the door of the open heart. No room for help from a kindly stranger. But the threat of harm from a greedy stranger could lever her.

She came back, a little pink around the edges, but carrying herself proudly and well. She slid onto the bench and said, "I wasn't babbling. I meant it . . . about the money."

"Can you afford a gesture that expensive?"

"I'm on a good salary. There's nothing I want so badly I

10

can't get along without it. But you have to keep your side of the bargain and leave me alone."

"Why is that so important?"

"A lot of people thought he was a very nice guy. I want to leave it that way. And I don't think I want to know any more than I know right now."

"I weaken a lot easier when I have the money in my hand, honey."

"Don't you believe me?"

"Let's go look at it. Or did you put it in a lock-box?"

She finished her sherry and put her glass down. "Any time you're ready, Mr. McGee."

"Trav."

She shrugged. "Trav, then. But there's not too much point in it. I don't plan to get to know you. I don't think Mike would want me to know you. I don't think he knows you."

"He used to. But people change."

"He shouldn't have guessed about the money. I started to tell him. I wish he hadn't guessed."

I finished my drink, beckoned for the check. "It brought me to you at a dead run, Miss Nina."

"How marvelous for me!"

two

SHE HAD a third-floor walkup on 53rd, a few doors from Second Avenue, a studio apartment with one bedroom. The hallway had a girlie flavor, hints of soap and perfume on the stale and dusty air. They tend to flock together. Once a few of them are established, they know when the next vacancy is coming up—and there is always a friend in need.

Nina Gibson was clean but not neat. Great stacks of decorator and craft and design magazines. Shelves of presentation designs that never quite worked out. A hugh drawing table with Luxo lamps clamped onto it, like big gray metal grasshoppers. Art books. Big action paintings, Kline-like, but without Kline's sober weight and dignity. A great big pushpin wall with her working drawings stuck all over it. A ratty, unhoused assortment of high-fidelity components.

When they get you into their nest and the door is closed, they stiffen up. It is one of the syndromes of the new freedom, I guess. Man and woman in the living place, in the food and bed place. This is my cave and I live here. Stiffness and exaggerated informality and the laughter goes Ha Ha, as if written down that way. And too much of silence between the very ordinary comments. This is because, I think, the living place, just being there, focuses the attention on sexual speculations. In the living place they tuck themselves in and walk carefully. How would we be together? It is the great unasked question. Eyes get a little shifty. Excuses are made in a lofty tone, and the special advantages are pointed out in the brass voice of a Greek guide describing the ruined temples.

Nina said, "Excuse the mess. I do a lot of work here."

I gave an unwelcome blurt of laughter. She stared at me as if I'd lost my mind. But I couldn't tell her about the wild Freudian slip I had suddenly remembered. Years ago I had taken a shy girl to dinner. She had eaten like a wolf pack, even to having a second piece of cocoanut-cream pie. I had

12

gone up to her place for the well-known nightcap. The girl she lived with was away for the weekend. We were feeling each other out, making chatty talk on one level, creating sensual tensions on another. I was deciding just when and how to make my pass, and she was wondering when it was coming and what to do about it—acceptance or rejection. She sighed and smiled and gave a little hitch to her skirt and said, "My goodness, I shouldn't have had that second piece of pants."

"Is something so terribly funny?" Nina demanded.

"No, I just . . ." I was saved by the telephone. She hurried to it and answered.

"Hello? Oh hi, Ben. What? No. No, I'm sorry, I guess not. No, dear, it isn't like that. I'm on two more accounts now, and there just doesn't seem to be any time."

Her voice went on, polite, personal, unswervingly firm in rejection of whatever pitch Ben was making. I wandered over to the push-pin wall and looked at her work. One drawing of a jar was striking. It had a severe and classic beauty. She hung up and came over to me.

"Do you like that one?" she asked.

"Very much."

"You've got a pretty good eye, McGee. The client didn't like it. We go around telling each other that good taste will sell. Maybe it will, at the right time and the right place. But what is truly commercial is a kind of vulgarity upgraded just enough to look like good taste. And the best ones in the business are the ones who can toss that kind of crap off naturally, and really believe it's great."

I looked down at her thoughtful face. "The trouble with that jar, Nina, what's there to put in it?"

"You have a point. Wait right here." She went into the small bedroom and closed the door. I prowled the place. I looked at the books and the records. Aside from an unwholesome taste for string quartets, and a certain gullibility about pre-digested sociology, she passed the McGee test with about a $B+$. Hell, an $A-$. Maybe somebody had given her the Vance Packard books. He has the profitable knack of making what everybody has known all along sound like something new and astonishing. The same way Norman Vincent Peale invented Christianity and James Jones designed the M-1 rifle. I could relate all three to her handsome jug. Theirs was an upgraded vulgarity.

She came out suddenly and marched across to me and put ten thousand dollars into my hand. I sat on her couch and bounced it in my hand and took the two rubber bands off it. Three packs of used bills in the bank wrappers, initialed by whoever had done the wrapping. Two packs of fifty fifties. One pack of fifty hundreds. She stood in her pale gray blouse and her suit skirt, in her dark pumps and her nylons and her discontent, and looked at me with a small defiant face. This was her gesture of disappointing love, and it seemed a shame to bitch it for her. I riffled the edges of the bills in silence, and snapped the rubber bands back on. I flipped the little brick of money at her head and she dodged wildly and stuck one hand up and surprised herself by catching it.

She stared blankly at me. "What's wrong?"

I swung my legs up and stretched out on her couch, fingers laced at the nape of my neck. "It's a pretty little egg, honey, but I want to meet the goose."

She stomped her foot. "You son-of-a-bitch!"

"It tempted me a little, but not enough. This goose seems to be named Armister."

"Get *out* of here!"

"Let's have a nice little talk."

In her fury she made an unwise lunge to yank me off the couch. I caught her wrists. She was a very strong little girl. She nearly got her teeth into my hand before I could get my forearm under her chin. She tried to kick, but she didn't have the room or the leverage. But she fought—grunting, writhing, flinging herself around until she landed in a sitting position, with a great padded thump, beside the couch. She slumped then, breathing hard in exhaustion, a tousle of the blue-black hair hiding one blue eye.

"Damn you!" she gasped. "Damn you, damn you, damn you!"

"Will you listen?"

"No!"

"It's all very simple. How about this guy, this wonderful marriageable Howard Plummer? What kind of a dreary excuse for a girl are you?"

"I'm not listening to you."

"The tiresome thing about you, honey, is that if he was still alive, you probably wouldn't listen to him either. Suppose you found the money and he was still alive. I can see the scene. Your eyes flash fire. Fists on your hips. A hell of a nasty tone of voice. Howie, darling, prove to me you're not a thief, and it better be good. Why, that poor slob really lucked out of marrying you, darling girl. Howie, darling, this little red smudge on your collar better be blood, you two-timing

14

bastard. Howie, baby, don't you take a step outside our happy home without letting me know where you are every single minute."

"You . . . you filthy . . ."

"You poor righteous little prude. Poor Miss Prim."

"What are you trying to *do* to me?"

"Make you give your man the same break any court would give him. Innocent until proven guilty. And the court wouldn't have gone to bed with him before condemning him without a trial, baby."

I released her wrists. She belted me a good one, and a micro-second after it landed, I jarred her down to her heels with an open-handed blow. The blue eyes swarmed out of focus and came back, shocked and wide, and then the tears hit her. They choked her and ripped her up, and she leaned into me, grinding her face into the side of my knee. I stroked her hair. It was all spasms, as convulsive as trying to steady a vomiting drunk. I wondered if she had really cried since her Howie had died. She was ridding herself of poison, coughing it out. It took her a long time to slow down and begin to ride it with any kind of reasonable rhythm. I got up and boosted her onto the couch and went off and found her bathroom, brought her back a cold wet washcloth and a big soft dry towel. I sat on the floor beside the couch and patted her once in a while. She drifted into a limp exhaustion, punctuated by a hiccup now and again. She sighed and turned her face toward me. I swabbed it with the cold cloth and she dried it on the towel. She stared at me, quiet and solemn as a justly punished child.

"Trav. Trav, I've been horrible."

"So?"

"Don't you see? I didn't even give him a chance. He couldn't explain, and I didn't even give him a chance."

"Do you understand that, Nina?"

"N-No."

"You had to muffle the pain any way you could. Lessen the loss. By trying to believe he lied and cheated. But you couldn't really believe it. It's a proof of how much love there was."

"But it's so unfair to him."

"Not to him, honey. To his memory, maybe. Not to him."

"What . . . what can I do now?"

"There's just one thing we can do. It's what I came to do. It's what Mike sent me to do. Let's find out what happened."

"But you made me think it was just the money that . . ."

I pushed her hair back away from the other puffy eye. "Mike said I might have to shake you up."

She stared at me. She shook her head slowly from side to side. She made a mouth. "You two. You and Mike. How could you know more about me that I knew?"

"Is it a deal?"

Her smile was frail, but it was a smile. "We'll have a lot of nice little talks."

After she regained enough energy to check the larder, she told me how far and in what direction I had to go to find a delicatessen. When I returned, she had changed to baggy slacks and a big pink hairy sweatshirt. She had fixed her face and her hair and set a table for us by the window. She unloaded the sacks, accusing me of exotic and extravagant tastes. But she found herself hungrier than she had expected. Her voice was still husky from her tears, and I had left a small bruise along her left jaw.

After we had eaten and she had stacked the few dishes, we sat on the couch with drinks.

"I didn't even know he had been killed until noon of the next day," she said in a soft thoughtful voice. "And I fell all apart. Those days are a blur. Sedatives, good friends standing by. I wanted to die too. It seemed such a horrid waste, to lose him that way. Sort of by mistake. Because somebody was greedy and scared and careless, some dirty sick animal out of nowhere. But I held myself together somehow. His sister flew out from California. There was a service here because of his friends here. She took care of his things, giving some away, giving me what she thought I'd like to have of his, closing his apartment. The body went back to Minnesota to be buried there in the family plot with his parents. I couldn't have stood going there and enduring another service. I think his sister understood. I hope she did. It wasn't until after she was gone that I remembered his things here. I was in such a daze. We weren't exactly living together. Just sort of. After we were married, we were going to live here and give up his apartment. It was handier for both of us. He had a key to here. And some personal things here. I didn't know exactly what he'd brought over. I'd already started taking up less room with my stuff to give him room. We knew what furniture of his we were going to bring over. I'd given him half my closet shelf. So finally I got the courage to go through the things he'd brought over, stopping every once in a while to lie down and cry myself sick. Over little things. I had to stand on a chair

16

to each the back of the shelf. The money was last. It was in the corner. It was wrapped in brown paper and tied with string. He died a week before my twenty-fourth birthday, Trav, and I didn't want to open it because I thought that if it was a gift for me hidden there, it would just break my heart so badly I'd never never get over it. I sat on the bed and unwrapped it . . . and it was the money. And suddenly there was a coldness in my heart, and I suddenly decided that he . . . that he . . ."

"Easy, Nina."

"When you think you know everything about a person and . . ."

"We both know it was a defensive emotional reaction."

"I wish I was as certain as you are, Trav. Maybe I am a lousy little righteous prude."

"And maybe we find out it was just what you thought it was."

She nodded. She slipped her hand into mine. "I know. I've thought of that. But now I know I do have to find out. And for that I have . . . I have to thank you. What should we do about the money?"

"We'll know later what has to be done. If it's all right with you, I'll take it along and put it in the hotel safe. Now tell me about his work."

In a little while she began yawning, and I knew she'd given all she had to give, for one day. She found a heavy manila envelope and I sealed the money into it. She came with me to the door and, sleepy as a child, unthinkingly lifted her face for a kiss. Her mouth was soft. She backed away suddenly and put her hand to her throat.

"I wasn't trying to be . . ."

"Go to bed, Miss Nina. Go to sleep. Dream good dreams."

"I might. I just might."

three

AFTER BREAKFAST I made some phone calls and found out which precinct I should contact. I went to the precinct and stated my wishes. They looked it up. Their man who had worked the case, along with the Homicide people who had covered it, was a Sergeant T. Rassko. I couldn't even find out that much until a Lieutenant Bree had questioned me with care and suspicion.

"I don't get the point," he kept saying, as he teetered and patted his stomach. "Whadaya tryna complish?"

I tried again. "Lieutenant, you know what a veteran is?"

"Don't get smart with me."

"This veteran is in a veterans hospital. Ever since Korea. Blind and busted up. Plummer was going to marry this veteran's kid sister. I'm the veteran's best friend. He asked me to find out how Plummer got killed."

"Whadaya tryna complish? It was in the papers. You want to make out we're not doing a job around here? You want to tell us something we don't know already. I don't get the point."

"Lieutenant, please, imagine that you are a blind veteran in a hospital. Your sister's fiance gets killed."

"Better than she should have married him, the one my sister married."

"Would you be satisfied with hearing somebody read you a little newspaper item, or would you want to have a friend go see where and how it happened and come and tell you about it?"

Comprehension began, twinkled, flowered into a smile. "Hey, you just want to tell him how it was covered, hey?"

"That's it."

"Let's see your identification again, McGee."

He studied my Florida driver's license. There is a space for occupation. It is a challenge to invention. This year I had written *Exectve* in the little box. As he handed it back, the cop-eyes took the practiced flickering inventory—tailoring, fabric, shirt collar, knuckles and fingernails, shoe shine, haircut—all the subtle clues to status.

"What kind of work you in, Mr. McGee?"

"Marine fabrications consultant."

"Yeah. You sit over there and I'll see what I can do." He walked heavily away, portly, white-haired, slow of wit. I sat on a worn bench and watched the flow of business. It is about as dramatic as sitting in a post office, and there are the same institutional smells of flesh, sweat, disinfectants and mimeo ink. Two percent of police work is involved with blood. All the rest of it is a slow, querulous, intricate involvement with small rules and procedures, violations of numbered ordinances, complaints made out of spite and ignorance, all the little abrasions and irritations of too many people living in too small a space. The standard police attitude is one of tired, kindly, patronizing exasperation.

Thomas Rassko, Detective Sergeant, looked and acted like a young clerk in a fashionable men's store. Quiet, bored, indifferent, quietly dressed, pale and cat-footed. Bree had cleared me, but I was obviously a waste of time. He led me to the visitor's chair beside a bull-pen desk, went away and came back with a thin file packet.

He sat down and opened it and sorted the contents and said, "Deceased white male American age twenty-seven. Estimated time of death, between eleven and midnight on Saturday, August tenth. The body was found just inside the truck driveway to a warehouse at three eighteen West Nineteenth Street. There was a notification by the warehouse watchman at one thirty-five." He sorted some eight-by-ten glossies and handed me one. "This will give you the best idea of it."

Howard Plummer lay in the harshness of the electronic flash, face down on asphalt, close to a brick wall. He was turned slightly toward the wall, legs sprawled loose, one arm under him, the jacket of his pale suit hiked above the small of his back. Both side pockets of his pants and one hip pocket were pulled inside out.

"You could practically call it accidental death," Rassko said. "A standard mugging that went wrong. The way they work it, there are usually two of them. They pick somebody well-dressed, maybe a little bit smashed, and follow along close, and when the situation is right, no traffic, and a handy dark corner, the stronger of the two takes him from behind, an

19

arm around the throat, yanks him into the dark corner, and the other one cleans him—wallet, watch, everything. By then, if he hasn't blacked out, they yank his pants down around his ankles, give him a hell of a shove and then run like hell. This Plummer was husky. Big enough to make them nervous, maybe. Or maybe he struggled too hard. Or maybe they were amateurs. Like sometimes we get sailors who get rolled and then try to take it back from anybody who comes along. That forearm across the throat can be very dangerous. They probably thought he had just blacked out, but the larynx was crushed. They let him drop and they ran, and he strangled to death."

"No leads at all?"

"This is a very low category of crime, Mr. McGee. Punk kids come in from way out—Queens, Brooklyn, even Jersey —so it isn't necessarily a neighborhood thing. Maybe they never even found out the guy died. They aren't newspaper readers. Our informants came up empty so far. There was nothing for the lab to go on. We couldn't find anybody who saw anything. We estimate he had about fifty dollars on him. His wallet never showed up. Nobody, not even his girl, could tell us the make wrist watch he was wearing, so we don't know if it was pawned."

"What was he doing in that neighborhood?"

Rassko shrugged. "It was a hot Saturday night. His girl had to go to some kind of a business dinner at a hotel. He left his apartment about six. We couldn't trace him. Maybe he was just cruising. We don't know whether he was walking east or west when he got hit. Maybe he took a girl home and he was walking looking for a cab. Too bad. Nice fellow, I guess, good education, good job and about to be married. Like I said, it's almost like accidental death. But it was no place for a well-dressed man to be walking alone at night, especially if he'd had a few drinks. That's asking for it."

"Did you have any trouble identifying him?"

"No. His name was written on the label in his suit, and the name was in the phone book. What we do to speed it up, we take a Polaroid flash of the face and send a man to check with the neighbors. The first contact verified the identity. I don't know where else we can go with it. Tomorrow or next year we may break somebody in connection with something else and hear all about this one, so we can close the file. There's only so much work you can do on a thing like this, and then it stops making sense to go further on account of the rest of the work load. But we don't forget it. We keep the live cases posted."

I thanked him for giving me so much time. I went out into the bright beautiful October day and walked slowly and thoughtfully back toward midtown. It was just past noon and the offices were beginning to flood the streets with a warm hurrying flow of girls. A burly man, in more of a hurry than I was, bumped into me and thrust me into a tall girl. They both whirled and snarled at me.

New York is where it is going to begin, I think. You can see it coming. The insect experts have learned how it works with locusts. Until locust population reaches a certain density, they all act like any grasshoppers. When the critical point is reached, they turn savage and swarm, and try to eat the world. We're nearing a critical point. One day soon two strangers will bump into each other at high noon in the middle of New York. But this time they won't snarl and go on. They will stop and stare and then leap at each others' throats in a dreadful silence. The infection will spread outward from that point. Old ladies will crack skulls with their deadly handbags. Cars will plunge down the crowded sidewalks. Drivers will be torn out of their cars and stomped. It will spread to all the huge cities of the world, and by dawn of the next day there will be a horrid silence of sprawled bodies and tumbled vehicles, gutted buildings and a few wisps of smoke. And through that silence will prowl a few, a very few of the most powerful ones, ragged and bloody, slowly tracking each other down.

I went back to my sterile cheerful miracle-plastic automated rectangle set high in the flank of a new hotel. I shucked my jacket and lay cradled on foam, breathing air made by careful machines, supine in a sub-audio hum that silenced all the city sounds.

I thought of death and money and blue-eyed tears. And some other blue eyes gone blind. This emotional obligation did not fit me. I felt awkward in the uncomfortable role. I wished to be purely McGee, that pale-eyed, wire-haired girl-finder, that big shambling brown boat-bum who walks beaches, slays small fierce fish, busts minor icons, argues, smiles and disbelieves, that knuckly scar-tissued reject from a structured society, who waits until the money gets low, and then goes out and takes it from the taker, keeps half, and gives the rest back to the innocent. These matters can best be handled by the uninvolved.

But I was involved in this. While Missy, neck-deep in the

21

steaming old stone bath, had been giggling and clasping Travis McGee within her sturdy little legs, somebody had blinded Mike Gibson and chopped him up.

I frowned at my sound-proofed ceiling and thought how they could improve the hotel service. Make the rounds—manager, technician and chambermaid. Are you happy enough, sir? Not quite. Gather around the bed, open the little compartment in the headboard, pull out the joy tubes and slip them into the veins, unreel the joy wires and needle them into the happy-making part of the brain. Adjust the volume. Is that better, sir? Enormously. When are you leaving us, sir? Turn me off next Tuesday. Thank you, sir. Enjoy your stay in New York, sir. Happy hallucinations.

I detected the reason for my reluctance to make the next move. I was afraid that, through ignorance, I would blow the whole thing.

And the next move was Robert.

Nina had told me that if I could make him talk to me, he could tell me more about Howard Plummer's job than anyone else. Robert Imber. He worked in the Trust Department of a Fifth Avenue bank.

Robert received me in a junior shrine of his very own, a leathery little church-lighted opaque box, filled with a hush of money. He sat waxen in his dark suit, his pale little mouth sucked in, a steep and glossy wave in his dark brown hair. No one had ever called him Bob or Bobby. He was a Robert, brown-eyed and watchful.

"Yes, a dreadful dreadful thing," he said. "This city is a jungle. I hope Miss Gibson is . . . recovering. I really hardly know her. You see, I left Armister-Hawes almost a year ago, and that was about the time Howard began to go with Miss Gibson."

"I don't yet understand what Armister-Hawes is."

He blushed as though caught in dreadful error. "It isn't *really* Armister-Hawes. It used to be, years ago. It was an investment banking house with branches in London and Brussels and Lisbon. But it is still in those same charming old offices, and the brass plate at the entrance says Armister-Hawes and one gets in the habit. Really, it's just the headquarters from which the Armister financial affairs are handled."

"They need a headquarters for that?"

"Oh yes indeed, Mr. McGee. And quite a large staff. It's very *old* money, and quite a bit of money. There are the

22

real estate holdings to manage, and quite a complex structure of holding companies, trusts, foundations, corporate investment entities, and several very active portfolios, of course. Charles McKewn Armister, the Fourth, as head of the present family, takes an active interest."

"Why did you leave?"

He studied me. He was so motionless, I wondered if he was breathing.

"I beg your pardon?"

"I wasn't trying to pry. I just thought it must have been very interesting work."

"Oh, it was. Excellent training, too. You get into so many ramifications of so many things. But this opportunity opened up for me. And there was the chance they wouldn't have been able to keep me on had I stayed. You see, I was junior to Howard Plummer."

"You mean they were cutting down?"

"Not exactly. It's rather difficult to explain it to a layman. They had embarked on a long-range program of cutting-down on active management responsibilities. For example, a large office building can mean a great deal of paper work, leases, maintenance contracts, tax matters and so on. They had begun to divest themselves of that sort of thing, a bit at a time. And they had begun to simplify the securities holdings, cutting down the number of transactions there too. And they had stopped going into new ventures."

"If that's the way it was going, I wonder why Howard didn't leave too."

"I have reason to believe he was considering it. But he was making quite good money. And he had a strong feeling of loyalty toward Mr. Armister. I imagine he would not have remained there much longer. He was a very sound man, Mr. McGee. Excellent investment judgment."

"Speaking as a layman, Mr. Imber, I wonder about one thing. If the policy changed, if they started selling off stuff, wouldn't it give somebody a better chance to siphon off some of that Armister money."

His eyes bulged. "What an extraordinary thing to say!"

"Wouldn't it be possible?"

"Surely you are joking, Mr. McGee. You have no idea of the impossibility of doing anything like that. There is a practically continuous tax audit of transactions. There are checks and balances within the accounting system. Mr. Armister is very alert. The head of the legal staff, Mr. Baynard Mulligan, is a very able and respected man. Mr. Lucius Penerra, head

23

of the accounting staff, is totally competent and respected. And *nothing* of any importance happens without Mr. Armister's personal investigation and approval. No, Mr. McGee, it is not only rather stupid to make a formless accusation like that, it could even be dangerous. I suspect it always is dangerous to slander any important and respected organization."

"There would be no way to clip that outfit?"

"Absolutely none. How did we get onto this subject?"

"One more question, Mr. Imber. Do you think the change of policy was smart?"

"That all depends."

"On what?"

"If you wish to take maximum advantage of a fortune of perhaps sixty or seventy millions of dollars, conserve it and increase it, while at the same time taking advantage of every tax break and every change in the economic climate, then the previous operation was better. But there are human values too. For example, Mr. Armister could have decided the work was too confining and restrictive. So he could seek a static rather than an active position. He might eventually have it in mind to cut down to the point where he could disband all operations and turn the holdings over to the trust departments of his banks. It might mean as much as a five percent change in his annual position, say three million dollars. That is what he would be in effect paying for the privilege of not taking risks."

"How old is he?"

"I would say he is about forty-four now. Inherited money is a terrible responsibility, Mr. McGee. It can become a crushing burden. Naturally I have no right to make guesses about what Mr. Armister wants or doesn't want."

"Did Howard ever complain about the new policy?"

"Why have you come to see me?"

"I wanted to find out about Howard's job."

"But why?"

"Miss Gibson is curious."

"Why should she be curious?"

"I wish I could tell you, Mr. Imber. But I gave my word."

"I certainly hope she isn't doubting Howard's honesty. He was a completely reliable man."

"Did he complain about the new policy?"

"Just once. Just before I left. Together we had worked out a very sound land-use program for a large tract in Maryland, and figured the investment needed to begin the first phase.

24

Then Mr. Mulligan told Howard they had decided to put it on the market. It was a bitter disappointment. Howard tried to fight the decision but got nowhere. I remember him walking back and forth in front of my desk, cursing the entire organization." He looked at his watch. "I'm very sorry, but ..."

I got up quickly. I thanked him for giving me the time. His handshake was abrupt, cold and strenuous. I glanced back at him as I went out his doorway. He was sitting erect, registering disapproval. I had slandered one of his gods. I was a reckless layman. And I suspected that he was annoyed with himself for talking perhaps too much and too freely. There is only one way to make people talk more than they care to. Listen. Listen with hungry earnest attention to every word. In the intensity of your attention, make little nods of agreement, little sounds of approval. You can't fake it. You have to really listen. In a posture of gratitude. And it is such a rare and startling experience for them, such a boon to ego, such a gratification of self, to find a genuine listener, that they want to prolong the experience. And the only way to do that is to keep talking. A good listener is far more rare than an adequate lover.

I had one useful source of information, if she was in the city. Constance Trimble Thatcher, age about seventy-two. She was the victim in a Palm Beach episode a few years ago. Though she was abnormally shrewd, a plausible sharpster had probed for a weak point and gouged her without mercy. I had discovered the con almost by accident, shaken it out of the operator and taken it all back to her and explained my fee system. She had turned over half without a murmur, demanding only that I never let anyone know what a damned old fool she had been.

I gave my name and she came to the phone in person and demanded that I come see her immediately before her extremely dull cocktail guests arrived. I taxied up to her big old duplex overlooking the park. I waited in the foyer. The tall old rooms were full of Regency furniture, gold brocade and fresh flowers. From the buffet preparations, I could guess she expected at least fifty.

She came trotting toward me, all smiles and pearls, piled white hair, green gown and little yips of welcome. She pulled me into a small study off the foyer and closed the mahogany door. She held my hands and peered up at me and said,

"McGee, McGee, you beautiful shifty scoundrel, if *only* I were thirty years younger."

"It's good to see you again, Mrs. Thatcher."

"What!"

"It's good to see you again, Connie."

She drew me over to the couch and we sat down. "I can't hope that you came to see an old lady just out of affection and old times, McGee. So there's something you want. And by the look of you, you haven't settled down yet and never will. You are a brigand, McGee."

"You never found me a nice girl, Connie."

"I sent you one, dear. But that was only for therapy."

"How is Joanie?"

"Back with her husband, but you would know that, wouldn't you, because it was your advice, so she told me. She's had her third child by now. Happy, they say. Was I a wicked old woman to send her to you?"

"You know you were."

"She needed a fling, and she could have fallen among thieves. She came back all aglow, McGee. I was eaten with jealousy. Tell me, what intrigue are you mixed up in now, and will you make any money?"

"What do you know about Charles McKewn Armister, the Fourth?"

She stared at me, head slightly cocked, one eye narrowed. It is easy to see how beautiful she must have been. "It's an interesting question," she said. "I know what there is to know."

"Which is why I came to you."

"When I was a little girl I fell off a horse—one of many many times—and his grandfather picked me up. And for a time I thought I would marry his father, a romantic fellow much given to kissing and writing love poems. But young Charlie has always been a stick. He was a very proper little boy. He married young. I think they were both twenty. Joanna Howlan he married. Money to money. They had summer places close together at Bar Harbor. A proper girl for him, I guess. One of those sturdy freckled girls, good at games, with a nice smile, and as proper as he. Two children of the marriage, a boy and a girl. The boy is twenty-two I would guess, and off in some far place in the Peace Corps, the girl eighteen and in Holyoke." She scowled into space. "I don't know how to say it, McGee. Charlie and his wife have no flair for the use of money, at least not that much money.

It's the cult of simplicity. They take all the magic out of it. Some kind of inverted snobbism, I guess. Social guilt. I just don't know. They have the old place on the Island, and an apartment in town and a smallish place at Hobe Sound. They are quiet, gentle, careful, dull people, and like I said, very good at games. Tennis and sailing and such. Charlie works very hard, they say, tending the money, making it grow and giving it away properly. It's strange we should mention a fling before, because I hear that Charlie is having himself one."

"Hmmm?"

"At the time of life when you can most expect it from a man who marries young, McGee. He had some kind of a breakdown a year ago. One of those anxiety things. Now he and Joanna are separated, but no one has said anything about divorce. He has his own apartment in town now. And he has created a drunken fuss in a few public places, bless him, after years of restraint. And I did hear something strange about the menage he's set up for himself." Her eyes clouded. "Let me think. When a woman forgets gossip, McGee, she is nearing the end of her road. What *was* it? Oh! I heard he is living with his lawyer and his secretary. Now *there* is a lurid arrangement for you!" She shook her head. "How could I have forgotten, dear boy? It might be handy though. He would be right there to prepare releases, wouldn't he? The lawyer is Baynard Mulligan. I've met him. Quite amusing and attractive, really. A rather nice Virginia family, but I understand they lost their money when he was small. Let me see now. He married Elena Garrett when he was thirty and she was no more than nineteen. But it didn't work out at *all*. It lasted four years, I think. They say she became alcoholic. Now she's married to some little teacher person over at Princeton, and has become very earnest and happy and she's having child after child. Baynard didn't remarry. Let me see what else I know about Charlie Armister."

"You are fantastic, Connie, and I am grateful, but for the last five minutes I've heard your guests arriving."

"McGee, darling, the bar is in a perfectly obvious place, and this is a hideously boring batch, actually the sort of party I'd have the Armisters at, if they were together and in the city. I get all the dead ones together and let them amuse each other. It's better than inflicting them in little dabs on my lively friends. I'll go out there when I'm ready. Perhaps the most interesting thing about Charlie Armister is his sister-

27

in-law. Joanna's elder sister. Give me a moment and I can tell you the exact name. Teresa Howlan Gernhardt . . . ah . . . Delancy Drummond. Terry she is called. Very international, and she's a charming earthy bawd, and has a marvelous figure for her age. She must be forty-six. She's usually in Rome or Athens, but I've heard she's here now, probably to hold her sister's hand. It's remarkable two girls could be so unlike. McGee, darling, I do suppose you are brassy enough to go ask Terry about Charlie, and she's probably annoyed enough to tell you. Where would she be? Mmmm. Either at the Plaza or at the Armister apartment. Try them both, dear. But don't get the wrong apartment. The old one, the one where she'd be, is the one on East Seventy-ninth. I think Charlie's hideout is further down. Now, I think I must go join my guests, much as I dread it. And you *must* come back and tell me the scandalous reason why you should be interested in Charlie Armister. I won't tell a *soul*."

"The hell with Charlie. I'm interested in that secretary." We stood up. I bent and kissed her soft wrinkled cheek.

"Slip out swiftly, my dear, before any of these old battle-wagons can clutch you and start honking at you. And phone me again soon."

I went out, smiling. The old elevator was rattling up the shaft so I took the stairs down. Constance Trimble Thatcher has her own kind of wisdom. There had been one morning when I had thought she had lost her mind. That was the morning Joanie had appeared at my gangplank looking pallid and jumpy and sacrificial in her resort wear. With trembling hand she had thrust a note at me. I saw her chin shaking as I looked at her after reading it. It was in Connie's oversized purple script, and all it said was, "Be very sweet to this dear exhausted harried child. Some utter idiots wanted to clap her into a rest home. But, as her godmother, I think I know better what she requires." The next day I had cast off and gone chugging down to the Keys bearing my wan, huddled, jittery passenger. Three weeks later I delivered her to the Miami airport for her flight back. She was ten pounds heavier, brown as walnuts, her hair bleached three shades lighter, her hands toughened by rowing, her muscles toned and springy. We kissed the long humid goodbys, and she laughed and cried—not in hysterics, but because she had good reasons for laughing and good reasons for crying, and we both knew just how she could pick up the pieces of her life and build something that would make sense. Captain McGee. Private cruises. Personalized therapy. And a little twinge of pain when the plane took off, pain for McGee, because she was too close to what-might-have-been. If there's no pain and no loss, it's only recreational ,and we can leave it to the minks. People have to be valued.

four

I DISCOVERED that Mrs. Drummond was in residence at the Plaza, but not in on this early Friday evening, so I took a taxi over to East 53rd. Nina was not home from the office. I whisked the soot off the wall by the entrance steps and sat and waited for her, and watched the office people bring their anxious dogs out. You could almost hear the dogs sigh as they reached the handiest pole. There was a preponderance of poodles.

This is the most desperate breed there is. They are just a little too bright for the servile role of dogdom. So their loneliness is a little more excruciating, their welcomes more frantic, their desire to please a little more intense. They seem to think that if they could just do everything right, they wouldn't have to be locked up in the silence—pacing, sleeping, brooding, enduring the swollen bladder. That's what they try to talk about. One day there will appear a super-poodle, one almost as bright as the most stupid alley cat, and he will figure it out. He will suddenly realize that his loneliness is merely a byproduct of his being used to ease the loneliness of his Owner. He'll tell the others. He'll leave messages. And some dark night they'll all start chewing throats.

A six-foot girl walked slowly by leading a little gray poodle in a jeweled collar. He peered out at me from under his curls with his little simian eyes. She wore flowered stretch pants and a furry white sweater. She slanted a quick look of speculation at me. She went by. Her haunches moved with a weighty slowness in time to her strolling gait. The poodle stared back at me. Bug off, he said. There isn't enough love to go around. You are the familiar enemy.

"Classy neighborhood, huh?" Nina said.

I sprang up and said, "You sneaked up on me."

"We call that one the Snow Maiden. She has about forty sweaters. All tight. All white."

"It's a lot of girl."

"Waiting long? Come on up."

As we slowly climbed the stairs, she said, "I slept like a felled ox, Trav. I didn't even hear the alarm. And all day I've been just dragging around. If I'd put my head down for one minute, I'd have gone to sleep. Reaction or something."

"You blew a lot of old fuses last night."

"And burned out the wiring." She leaned against the wall and handed me her key, and yawned. I let us in. The place was more orderly.

"Housework?" I said.

"A little bit last night. It was messy."

"I'll take you out to dinner tonight."

"Let me get out of my shoes and have a drink and think about it, dear. Fix me bourbon on ice, will you? You know where the things are. Knock and hand it in. A shower might wake me up."

"No sherry?"

She gave me a rueful smile. "I was on sherry because I was scared of what anything stronger would do to me. I was afraid of losing control. I'm a bourbon girl from way back."

She dragged her way into the bedroom and closed the door. I fixed drinks. When I rapped on the bedroom door, nothing happened. I could hear the shower. I went into the bedroom. Her clothing had been tossed on her unmade bed. The bathroom door was ajar. The shower roared. There was a warm, steamy, flowery scent of girl. I knocked on the bathroom door. In a moment a wet arm came out. I put the glass in the hand. It went back in.

"Thank you," she called. "You know what?"

"What."

"I'm getting a bonus."

"That's nice."

"On the Marvissa account. We got it. They took my design. It was a competition. Five hundred dollars."

"Congratulations."

"And I was so tired, my only response was a weak and humble little smile. I'll be out in a few minutes, dear."

I went back into the living room. The heady scent of soapy girl seemed to follow me out. I ordered McGee to stop picturing her in the shower. I told him he had seen whole platoons of showering women, and scrubbed many a glossy back in his day, and this was a damned poor time for adolescent erotic fantasies. And the business of the drink had not been a tricky invitation. It had been a friendly innocence. This was Mike's kid sister. It would have a flavor of incest. And this wasn't what he had meant by shaking her up. So I paced and smirked woodenly at her drawings, and wrenched my mind into other patterns.

At last she came out in feathery slippers and a long pink and black robe cinched tightly around the tininess of her waist, with a little mist of perspiration on her upper lip, and some of the ends of the blue-black hair dampened.

"I'll dress when we decide what kind of a place we're going."

"Sure. Refill?"

"Please."

So with new drinks, we sat and I told her about my day, Sergeant Rassko and Robert and Constance Trimble Thatcher. I made it complete. The Rassko thing was obviously a strain for her, so when I came to Robert I funnied him up more than he merited, and made her laugh a little. She was intrigued with Connie, and with the idea that so social and lofty a lady would be so gossipy with me.

"You must have some special credentials, Trav."

"I did her a favor once when she was very depressed. Her self-esteem was at a low ebb. She doesn't know many people like me. I guess I amuse her. And in some funny way, we're alike."

"You and Constance Trimble Thatcher?"

"We're both impatient with fraud. With all pretentious and phoney people. She can afford to be. With me it's an extravagance."

"Am I phoney?"

"You design the vulgar pots and sell them to the vulgar people. When you start believing them, you become fraudulent, Miss Nina. You make a plausible adjustment to the facts of life. I don't. And that isn't a virtue on my part. It's the disease of permanent adolescence. Honey, when you take your tongue out of your cheek, you become suspect."

"The Marvissa containers are hideous."

"Of course."

"But I'm proud of the bonus, Trav."

"Why not? Nina, once you accept the terms of the compromise, you'd be a damn fool not to do your best within those limitations. Beat them at their own game, and be proud you can."

"Okay, sir."

"Now. More questions about what Howie told you about the thievery."

"I told you, he only suspected it. He was very troubled about it. He said he couldn't prove anything. I asked him why not. He said I would have to take a course in accounting before he could even begin to explain it to me. But he tried to explain it. He said suppose you have a hundred buckets full of water and a hundred empty buckets, and all of a sudden you start pouring water back and forth from one to another as fast as you can. He said you could keep it moving around so fast that nobody would ever notice there was less and less total water all the time, and the only way it could be checked would be to stop the whole thing and carefully measure what was left."

"How about names?"

"He didn't like to talk about it to me. I'd always start pleading with him to quit. I kept telling him that if there was something nasty going on, he might get blamed or something. And I told him it was making him gloomy."

"What did he say about quitting?"

"He said that it was a good idea. In a little while. It irritated him that he couldn't sit down and have a serious talk with Mr. Armister. When he first went with them he said they used to talk things over, discuss future planning and so on. He said Mr. Armister had sound ideas. But then Mr. Armister got sort of . . . hearty and cheerful and indifferent. He said it had to be some kind of a high-level conspiracy, and he used to wonder if Mr. Armister was engineering it somehow, draining money out and hiding it away maybe in Switzerland for tax evasion reasons. He said he guessed he was getting too nosy, because Mr. Mulligan kept hinting that it might be a good time for Howie to locate somewhere else, with a nice bonus and good letters of commendation."

"But he never found anything specific."

"Not that I know of."

"And what was he going to do if he did? Did he say?"

"No. But he used to look very grim and angry, as if he would go to the authorities or something if he found out. I loved him, Trav, but I have to say that Howie was just a little bit stuffy. He had very rigid ideas of right and wrong. He was . . . sort of repressed." She blushed slightly. "I believed that after we were married, I could sort of loosen him up."

I leaned back and said, "Sixty to seventy millions is a lot of water to pass from bucket to bucket. Quite a lot could

33

get spilled. Ten percent would be six or seven million. Would you happen to know the name of the affectionate secretary?"

"Sure. Bonita Hersch. Howie couldn't stand her. She was Mr. Mulligan's secretary until Mr. Armister's secretary retired, and then she moved up."

"Why did he dislike her?"

"I guess because things changed there after she became Mr. Armister's secretary. You know how offices are. Or do you? They can be nice, everybody getting along, or it can get very formal. She built a wall around Mr. Armister and set the other people against each other. Trav?"

"Yes, Miss Nina."

"What do you *really* think about all this?"

I turned and looked into the intent blue eyes, thicketed with those long lashes, at the face small and young under the weight of blue-black curls.

"I think it is a lot of money. We're all still carnivorous, and money is the meat. If there's a lot of money and any possible way to get at it, I think people will do some strange warped things. Hardly anybody is really immune to the hunger, not if there's enough in view. I know I'm not."

"Is that one of those facts of life you were lecturing me about?"

"I was patronizing you, baby. I do a lot of talking. It makes me believe sometimes I know who I am. McGee, the free spirit. Such crap. All I've ever done is trade one kind of bondage for another. I'm the victim of my own swashbuckled image of myself. I'm lazy, selfish and pretty shifty, Miss Nina. So I have to have an excuse structure. So I glamorize my deficiencies, and lecture pretty little women about truth and beauty. Are you wise enough to understand that? If so, you are wise enough not to trip over my manufactured image."

"I think you are very strange."

"Don't get intrigued. It's not worth it. I'm a high level beach-bum. And I'm about as permanent as a black eye."

There is a time in all such things when eyes look into eyes, with vision narrowing and intensifying until there is nothing left but the eyes, searched and searching. This is a strange and tingling thing that narrows the breath—but it is a communication, and once it has happened there is an awareness beyond words.

She licked a dry mouth and half-whispered, "I've run into doors. I've had my share of black eyes. I've gotten over them."

"Shut up."

"Mike said you were such a hell of a fine soldier."

"The result of a pertinent observation. I noticed that the better you were, the longer you lasted. Out of pure fright, I put my heart into it."

"Mike said you were going into business with your brother when you got back."

"When I got back, there wasn't any business. They had taken it away from him, and he had worked too hard at it, and he killed himself."

Blue eyes came closer and the voice was more of a whisper. "Mike said you have a strange thing about women."

"I happen to think they are people. Not cute objects. I think that people hurting people is the original sin. To score for the sake of scoring diminishes a man. I can't value a woman who won't value herself. McGee's credo. That's why they won't give me a playboy card. I won't romp with the bunnies."

With her lips two inches from mine and her lids looking heavy, she said, "Mike said it's a disaster to play poker with you."

"I live aboard my winnings. It's called the Busted Flush."

"Take me for a boat ride," she said, and rested her fists against my chest and fitted a soft sighing mouth to mine. It started in mildness, and lifted swiftly to a more agonizing sweetness of need than one can plausibly expect from a kiss. Her arms pulled, and she gave a wrenching gasp, and I held her away. She stared, blind and wide, then plunged up and wandered away, went over to her push-pin wall and began idly straightening drawings.

"Trav?"

"We have to decide where to eat so you can get dressed."

"Trav?"

"Go; with the basic black, something suitable for baked mussels, pasta, a big garlic salad ice-cold, a bottle of Bardolino, espresso."

"Trav, damn it!"

"And shoes you can walk in, because we'll want to walk a little while after dinner and look at the lights and look at the people."

She turned and looked at me and shook her head in a sad exasperation and went into the bedroom and closed the door.

I held it all off until we were down to the second cups of

the thick bitter coffee. I held it off by regaling her with folksy legends of the palm country, and bits of marina lore—such as my neighbor boat which housed the Alabama Tiger's perpetual floating house-party, and how to catch a snook, and the best brand of rum in Nassau and such like. I paused for a moment.

"Trav?" she said, in that same old tone of voice, and I was locked into the intensity of her blue eyes and we were back with it.

"As you told me in the beginning, you are a darling girl. And a darling vulnerable girl because somebody dimmed your lights back on August tenth, and because last night you whooped and coughed up enough of yourself to be equivalent to ten sessions on the couch and you want to transfer to me more than you should. You are just too damned willing to give all that trust and faith and affection, and it scares me. And when a damn fool shoots fish in a barrel, he also blows hell out of the barrel."

"Is that all?"

"When I think of more, I'll let you know."

"I don't need a den mother. I can take my own risks. For my own reasons."

"Just like a grownup?"

"Oh shush. You don't do my vanity much good, McGee."

"Concentrate on your five-hundred-dollar bonus."

After long thought she gave a little shrug of acceptance. "So be it, den mother. What's your Saturday program?"

"Charlie Armister's sister-in-law. Terry Drummond. And hope to pick up some guide lines from her. Ready? Let's take that walk."

We walked a long amiable way on Fifth, making small jokes that seemed funnier than they probably were, and nightcapped with George at the Blue Bar at the Algonquin, and then taxied her home and held the cab. "Coward," she whispered, and gave me a child's simple kiss, and started up the stairs with a great burlesque comic show of exaggerated hip waving, turned and waved and grinned and hurried on up.

five

I CALLED Mrs. Drummond again on the house phone at ten minutes of eleven and she told me to come up. There was a man with her in the sitting room of the small suite. He had wire glasses, a tall forehead and a deferential manner. She introduced him as Mr. King.

"What do you want to talk to me about?" she asked. She was tall and slender, and brown as a Navajo. She had dusty black hair pulled back into a careless bun. She wore tailored gray slacks, gold strap-sandals, a silk shirt with three-quarter sleeves in an unusual shade of gray-green which enhanced the vivid and astonishing green of unusually large eyes. Her figure, as advertised, was taut and trim, tender and tidy as a young girl's. Even the backs of her slender hands were young. But the years had chopped her face. It was creased and withered and eroded into a simian brownness out of which the young green eyes stared. She had a deep drawling voice, barked rough by whisky and smoking and living. She was smoking a cigarette, and her habits with it had a masculine look.

I glanced at King. She said, "Mr. King would like to know too."

Sometimes you have to take the risk very quickly, before you can scare yourself. "I want to know what's happening to Charlie Armister."

"Why, dear?"

"As a favor for a friend. And maybe, in all the confusion, some of that money will rub off on me."

"So you want to hustle him, dear?"

"Not to the exclusion of everything else, Mrs. Drummond." She turned to King. "You can pop along now, sweetie."

"But I think I should . . ."

"Please."

"But in view of what he . . ."

37

She moved to him in a slow graceful stride, patted his cheek, took his shoulder and turned him toward the door. "I'll be in touch."

He went with an obvious reluctance. She went over and sat on a small desk, slim legs swinging. She gave me her monkey grin.

"He's my lawyer. He's terribly protective. People get some terribly cute ideas, and I like to have him nearby when I make my little appraisal."

"Do I look that harmless?"

"No indeed, ducks. But old Connie Thatcher gave me a ring and said that if you should happen to come see me, you're a dear, and I should be nice. I was afraid you'd be one of those nice young men. I shouldn't underestimate Connie. She called you a brigand. Fix me a drink, dear. Two fingers of the Plymouth gin. One cube."

She watched me in silence as I fixed it and took it over to her. When I handed it to her, she caught me by the wrist with her free hand. Her fingers were thin and hot and strong. I automatically resisted her attempt to turn my wrist. She released me at once and grinned at me. I had the feeling I had won a claiming race, and before making her bid she had taken a look at my teeth.

"You're a powerful creature, Trav. Connie said people call you that. Please call me Terry. Aren't you drinking?"

"Not right now, thanks."

"I've offended you, haven't I?"

"Give me the blue ribbon and they can lead me back to my stall."

Her laugh was deep. "What would you expect of me, sweetie? Coyness, for God's sake? I'm a vulgar honest woman inspecting prime male. I don't see too many of your breed. They're either pretty boys or dull muscular oxen or aging flab. You move well, McGee. And I like deep-set gray eyes, hard stubborn jaws and sensuous mouths. Aren't you a girl-watcher?"

"Of course."

"I'm too old for you, sweetie. But not too old to think of taking you to bed." She stuck a finger in her drink and stirred it and licked her finger. "Didn't Connie tell you I'm notoriously crude?"

"You certainly work at it, Terry."

For an instant the vivid green eyes narrowed, and then she laughed. "I'm supposed to be keeping *you* off balance, sweetie. It isn't supposed to work the other way."

"So let's call it a draw. I'm an acceptable stud, and from the neck down you're Miss Universe. And if there was ever any reason to go to bed, we'd probably find each other reasonably competent. But I came here to talk about Charlie."

"You *are* a bold bastard, aren't you?"

"Sure. And we're both emotional cripples, Terry. I've never married and you can't stay married, so perhaps all we've got is competence. And that makes a hell of a dry diet. Now how about Charlie?"

She sprang down from the desk, gave me a tearful savage glare, and ran into the bedroom and slammed the door as hard as she could.

I wandered over to the bar table and fixed myself a weak drink. I took it to the window and stood and watched the Saturday people strolling on the park walks. I picked through the magazines on the coffee table, and sat and leafed through one. There were some excellent color reproductions of three recent paintings by Tapies, work that had the burned, parched, textured, solemn, heartbreak look of his native Spain. I lusted to own one. I told myself I could bundle monkey-face into the sack and use her up, and she'd buy me one as a party favor. And she could buy all my clothes. In no time at all I too could look like a fag ski instructor. She could trundle me off to Athens. Teresa Howlan Gernhardt Delancy Drummond McGee. I wondered how many hours a day it cost her to keep that figure in such superb condition. Diet, steam, massage, exercise, lotions, hormones, dynamic tension. And lotsa lovin'—that most effective suppling agent of all. From the neck down she was Doriana Gray, dreading the magic moment when, overnight, every excess would suddenly become visible.

In twenty minutes she opened the door cautiously and stared out at me, brown face slightly puffed. "Oh," she said.

"Should I have left?"

"Don't be an idiot."

"Two fingers and one cube?"

"Please." She sat in a wing chair by the windows. I took her the drink. She looked up at me with a wan smile. "You know, McGee, you are sort of a walking emetic. You are a big rude finger down my throat."

I smiled at her. "You wouldn't settle for a standoff. You had to keep prodding, Terry."

"Okay. Now you're the dominant male. Now you're in charge. But people just don't talk to me like that."

"Because you're rich. Everybody you meet gives a damn about that. The rich are an alien race."

"And you don't give a damn?"

"Of course I do. But I can't con you and lick your pretty sandals simultaneously, honey."

"My God, you really and truly make me feel like a young girl again, Trav."

"It should be a relief to you to be able to drop the act you put on."

"I guess it is. Sort of. But what do I do for defense?"

"You go all demure."

"Jesus!" She gave her barking laugh. "Okay. We're friends. And if I'm not good at it, it's because I don't have many, and the ones I have are women." She held her hand out. I shook it. I sat on the couch. "Now we can talk about Charlie," she said.

"It will be a different kind of talk than it would have been."

"You're that smart too, aren't you? I mean smart in that way. Son of a gun. Charles McKewn Armister, the Fourth. He and my sister Joanna are the same age. And sort of the same kind of sturdy quiet smiling people. Built solemn sand castles. When they were twelve, thirteen, fourteen, in that range, she crewed for him, and they took about every cup the club put up. In tennis doubles they were almost unbeatable. Everybody knew they would be married and have healthy beautiful children, and everybody was right. I was a slimy child, two years older. When he was sixteen and I was eighteen, I tried to seduce him. I didn't really want him. It was just mischief. He always seemed sort of sexless to me. Maybe I was just curious. It took Charlie a hell of a long time to figure out what I was trying to do, and when the light dawned, he was aghast. He panicked. He fled. I thought I was terribly wicked that summer. I was merely silly and unhappy and reckless. And notorious. I had to buy an abortion in Boston, and got septic, and damn near died, so I wonder who that baby would have been, and who the others would have been if I could have had them. But this isn't about Charlie, is it?

"Back to Charlie. I never saw much of Charlie and Joanna. In my cluttered lousy life they seemed to be a nice far-off focus of sanity. I was the wild Howlan sister and she was the tame one. So now she sits stunned out there in that ugly gray castle on the Island, wondering if he's ever coming back. I go out there and get her drunk and make her talk it out.

It always looked like such a terribly *normal* marriage. But it wasn't. I mean I would have thought Charlie would have been one of those bluff types, a cheerful clap on your haunch and seven minutes later they're snoring like a bison. I was married to one of those, God help me. He had about the same attitude toward sex as he had toward breakfast. He didn't particularly care what was served as long as he could have a healthy breakfast that didn't take too damned long. But my weepy drunken sister at last tells me that Charlie was hexed, probably by his cruel, romantic, cold son-of-a-bitch of a father, just as I was by mine, but in the opposite direction. Charlie is all tied up in psychopathic knots about sex. Impotent a lot of the time. Scared of being impotent. Able to manage it only when he's very tired or slightly drunk. And they are so good and so dear to each other in all other ways. And such a healthy outdoorsy pair.

"A year ago he had a genuine breakdown. It was kept pretty quiet. He went into a private rest home. When he got out, he just didn't go back to Joanna. She saw him a few times. He seemed perfectly cheery, and a little too loud, and he made silly jokes. He said he was taking another apartment in town. He told her the usual check would be deposited in her account every month, and she should keep on having all the bills sent to the office. But she couldn't pin him down. She couldn't really communicate with him."

"How long was he in the rest home?"

"Two months and a half."

"Did she go to see him there?"

"She was told it would be better if she stayed away. They said it was an acute anxiety neurosis. I've been trying to dig into this damn fool situation, and I've been here two weeks, and I *still* haven't been able to see him. He doesn't go to any of his clubs anymore. He's in a five-bedroom apartment on East Seventy-first. His personal attorney, Baynard Mulligan lives there with him. And his private secretary, Miss Bonita Hersch. They have a daytime maid, a live-in cook and a chauffeur. He spends a couple of hours every working day at the office. I've left a dozen messages for him to call me. Nothing." She got up and went to the bar table and fixed herself another gin and ice.

She brought it over and sat beside me, turned to face me.

"Now I've made a damn fool of myself by telling a lot of very personal and private matters to an absolute stranger."

"But you stopped short."

"Did I?"

41

"Terry, you told the facts and left out the assumptions."

"Do I have to know how you fit into all this?"

"Not really."

She nodded. "Then you tell me what I'm assuming."

"You've thought it all over. You're reasonably shrewd. And you've known practically from birth that you are a target for every sharpie who comes along. So you develop an instinct. You know that something is wrong. It all adds up to one thing. Some people have managed to move in on Charlie Armister. They have gotten to him. They own him. Did you ever see a lamprey?"

"A what?"

"It's an eel. It hides in the weeds in the bottom of a lake. Sometimes it has to hide a long time. When a fat lake trout comes by, the eel shoots up and fastens its round mouth with a circle of teeth into the white belly of the fish. The fish struggles awhile, then goes on about its business, with eel in tow. It swims and feeds and lives for a long time, but it keeps getting thinner and weaker. When it dies, the eel leaves it and goes back into the weeds."

"Mulligan?"

"And Hersch and the necessary corps of assistants. It has to be a big and very delicate conspiracy. This isn't a hit-and-run operation. This is a symbiotic relationship."

"Do you think that is *really* happening?"

"First, they are now and have been for almost a year, liquidating profitable operations and making no new capital investments. Secondly, a very earnest young man who worked there and who was doggedly trying to find out what was going on, got himself mugged and killed in an alley two months ago."

She stared at me. "Are you insane?"

"The greater the profit, the greater the risk."

"But . . . but if they've got Charlie, we should go to the police at once!"

"Sure. What do we say?"

"We . . . we accuse Baynard Mulligan of conspiracy."

"And have him arrested?"

"Of course."

"And if we could force an audit somehow, we'd find the books in perfect balance. We'd find that every decision they've made can be justified. And Charlie would probably be furious. Mulligan would bring nine kinds of civil action against both of us. You see, whatever is happening, it probably isn't against Charlie's will. You can't safely control an unwilling

42

man over a long period of time. They've hooked him on something and they've made him happy with it."

"Hooked him?"

"Maybe they've addicted him. For example, oral demerol. It's a synthetic hard drug and perhaps twice as addictive as heroin. It would keep him buzzing and happy as a clam and dependent on the only source he knows."

"How ugly! How terrible!"

"But that's only a guess. I'm just saying that it's possible. With an unlimited supply they could keep him in good physical shape for a long long time. Long enough to shake a lot of leaves off the money tree, Terry."

"You've scared the hell out of me, Trav."

"I meant to. I don't want you getting reckless. I want them nice and confident."

"When did you decide this was going on?"

"As you were telling me all about Charlie."

"That was the last piece to the puzzle?"

"No. There's a few to go."

"What are you going to do? I want to help."

"I look for the weak link, Terry. Somebody who knows about it, and can be made to talk about it. I don't know how you can help. The best thing you can do is keep absolutely quiet."

She pursed her lips and nodded. "Yes. Yes, of course. But did you just sort of . . . stumble onto this, Trav?"

"My best friend's sister was engaged to the boy who was killed."

"Oh."

"I'm not used to the big rich. You can be my guide."

I saw the monkey-grin again. "We're just like anybody else. Isn't that what Hemingway told Fitzgerald? We're just like anyone else, except we have more money. And I think you know how to handle us very nicely. Well, directly, if not nicely." She held her glass out to me. "More of the same please."

I fixed it and as I gave it to her, I looked carefully to see if there was any effect from the others. The green eyes were clear and alert. The mouth had not loosened.

This was an international witch. A special segment of show business. A millioned girl had briefed me once upon a time. It is the iceberg analogy. The real-and-true school just under the surface, invisible. Perhaps like Charlie and Joanna Armister in the years of togetherness. And like old Connie. So that the ones you see, the ones that do a little flapping on the

43

surface, they are the fringe kids. The almosts. The restless ones like Terry Drummond, and the dubious nobility, and the climbers, lounging on the far-away sun decks with their sexpot acquisitions of both sexes, squinting bored into the Rolleis of the social photographers. Farukers, my millioned girl called them, an in-group word for the ones who make vulgar and obvious uses of themselves and their money. So this green-eyed Terry was not quite classy. She had roamed too far and hard and wide, divorced too publicly, made too many scenes, kept her perennially girlish rump too busy. Once upon a time maybe there had been something touchingly lonely about her, a hidden vulnerability, but now it was so encapsulated by the scars of roaming that all she could do was fake the emotions she believed she should feel.

But she had lost no sensitivity to mood and opinion. She smiled and said, "Don't tell me you're that conventional, McGee."

"What do you mean?"

"Didn't I detect some dreary middle-class disapproval?"

"Middle-class curiosity."

"Darling, I've tried everything. Twice. Does that answer your question?"

The laugh was gutteral and the eyes as old as Egypt.

"I was only wondering how you drink so much gin and stay girlish."

"Oh, that! Heavens. These are the only calories I get, darling. I gave up eating long ago. Twice a day my maid, my treasure, blends up a great goopy mess of protein and mineral and vitamin things and I choke it down. I'm balanced, dear. I'm inured. I'm in a continuous state of glowing health, slightly tiddly, but entirely aware and useful. I'm going riding at three today. Could you join me? And going to Connecticut for the weekend. We should be back by Monday noon, dear. It would give us time to discuss this whole dreadful mess."

"Sorry. There's only one thing to discuss. How do we break into the magic circle? What's the starting point? What's the cover story?"

She pursed her lips and laid a slender finger against the side of her nose. "Mmmm. What if I asked the Hersch person to lunch with me? As a secretarial type, the idea might enchant her. I could plead with her to send Charlie back to my sister. My word, I could even try to bribe her and see what happens! What do you think, Trav?"

"I think it might be interesting. I might join you, ac-

44

cidentally. But can I trust you not to let her suspect that you suspect that she is helping Mulligan pick Charlie clean?"

"Are you asking me if I'm capable of intrigue, dear?"

"That's about it."

"McGee, darling, you are looking at the woman who invented the word. I can be so devious I can hardly stand it."

"Gin and all?"

"Gin and all. Once upon a time I pried my third husband loose from a greedy bit of fluff by marrying her off to my second husband's younger brother, and then got them both out of the way by getting a dear friend to offer him a job in Brazil, and nobody ever realized I had anything to do with it."

"Remarkable."

"If I can't handle some meaty obvious little stenographic person, ducks, I should turn in my uniform."

"Do you think you can set it up for Monday?"

"I shall try."

"What if she says no?"

She looked amused. "Dear boy, if you were a twelve-year-old outfielder and Mickey Mantle invited you to lunch, would you turn him down?"

"It's a point."

She arched herself slightly. "I've spent my life in the major leagues."

six

SATURDAY AFTERNOON I went and took a look at Armister's setup on East 71st. It was a relatively recent building, perhaps ten years old. It had a canopy, a doorman, shallow planting areas carefully tended, a reception desk, some pretentious pieces of bronze statuary in the paneled foyer. I did not loiter. In places like that, the residents pay for insulation. The staff has cold eyes. They have seen all the gimmicks, and know how to block them.

I found the right alley that led to the back of the building. A wide ramp led down to the basement parking area. I walked down the ramp. Big cars had a luxurious gleam under the ceiling lights. The service elevators were beyond a wire cage where an old man sat under a hooded light. Over in the wash rack, a Negro was slowly and carefully polishing a bottle-green Lancia.

"Can I help you?" the old man said.

"Yes, please. I'm supposed to pick up the Thayer's Mercedes. They told you about it."

"What?"

"The black 300 SL. It's supposed to be ready to go."

"Thayer?"

"That's right."

"Mister, you must have the wrong place."

"Isn't this one twenty-one?"

"Yes, but we got no Thayer in the house at all."

"I wonder if I could use your phone."

"Sure thing. Come around."

I looked up Nina's number. I knew she was working at the office. I dialed. I let it ring ten times and hung up.

"Now I don't know what to do," I said. "They're in the country and wanted me to bring the car out."

"You sure it's East Seventy-first, mister?"

"That's what I was told."

46

"You just got the wrong place."

"Maybe I could wait a few minutes and try again."

"No long-distance calls."

"Of course not."

Two young girls came out of the service elevator. The Negro backed the Lancia out of the rack and brought it up for them. He put the top down. They went droning up the ramp and away. A package delivery man came whistling in, greeted the old man, and went up the stairs to the service entrance to the foyer. I moved casually to the other side of the cage and looked at the parking chart with the slots labeled with the names of the users.

"You won't find Thayer on there," the old man said.

"You've convinced me of that, friend. Which Armister is this?"

"Mr. Charles Armister."

I spotted another slot labeled Mulligan, not far from the Armister slot. Both had the apartment number beside the name. 9A.

My inspection of the chart was making him uneasy. I tried my call again. I hung up and said, "This is ridiculous."

His house phone rang. He picked it up and said, "Garage. Yes sir. Right away, sir." He hung up and called to the Negro. "Dobie, run that Highburn Cad around front on the double." He turned to me and said, "If he can start it. They haven't used that thing in six weeks."

That's what you wait and hope for, the opening the other man makes.

"Unless you have a chauffeur, a car is a nuisance in this town."

"We got about fifteen chauffeur-driven here. They're the ones get the use."

The Cadillac moved up the ramp, belching, missing a little.

"But that takes a lot of money."

"There's money in this house, mister. A man would like to cry, the amount of money there is in this house. Just take that name that caught your eye, that Armister. He could have ten chauffeurs and it wouldn't cramp him."

"But he struggles along with one, eh?"

"That's right. He's got Harris, the meanest son of a bitch I ever . . ." He stopped abruptly, hearing himself talk too much. He narrowed his eyes. "Isn't there any address for Thayer in that book?"

"Unlisted number."

47

He shifted in his chair. "They don't like people hanging around here, mister."

"Okay. Thanks for your help."

"Good luck to you."

I walked all the way down to Nina's Park Avenue office building. It had an echoing Saturday silence. I had my choice of automatic elevators. The music was turned off. After I had pounded on the corridor door a few times, a scrawny, smocked redhead let me in. She was smoking a small cigar. She led me back to Nina, to the cluttered workrooms where squeeze bottles germinate. Nina had a smutch on her chin. WQXR was blasting over a table radio—something dry, stringy and atonal. I watched her work until she told me I made her nervous, and then I went off and drank tepid beer out of paper cups with the redhead, and we talked about new realism, using bad words.

Nina gathered me up and we went out into a day which had turned colder, the late afternoon sunlight showing a watery weak threat of winter. We went to the hotel lounge where we had first talked, and because we had become different people to each other, it made it a different place. It was nearly empty. We sat at a curve of the padded bar. My bourbon girl, unsmutched, with eyes of finest blue.

It astonished me that she could not get enough of Teresa Howlan Gernhardt Delancy Drummond. Voice, hair, clothing, every nuance of conversation. "*You* said *that* to *her!*" Horror. Consternation.

At first it amused me, and then it irritated me. "She didn't step down from Olympus, honey. She's just another restless woman, that's all. She never had to grow up. She was one hell of an ornament for a long time. Now not so much. And when there's no more studs, there'll be nothing left but green eyes, money and gin. She's going to be a very tiresome, bad-tempered old woman."

"Why do you have to try to cut her down?"

"I'm not. Nina, really, don't act like a schoolgirl reading about a movie queen. Terry isn't worth that kind of awe."

"Stop patronizing me. Maybe I don't have your advantages, McGee. I'm just a simple thing from Kansas with a degree from Pratt Institute. I'm naive about the glamorous figures I read about in the papers."

"What are we quarreling about?"

"Just because I have a perfectly understandable curiosity . . ."

48

"She wore an emerald as big as a tea bag."

"What? With slacks?"

"In her navel, honey."

She stared at me and then laughed abruptly. "Okay, Travis. You win. I'll try to stop acting awed."

Cocktail-lounge business began to improve. I told her about checking the Armister apartment house, about all the careful insulation provided for the residents. We went out into the cool blue dusk and walked to her place. As we walked we made plans. I couldn't see any way to move any faster on the whole situation. I would wait for Terry's lunch with Bonita Hersch. So we had a Saturday night, and I would wait at her place while she changed, and then we would go to my hotel and I would leave her in one of the cocktail lounges while I changed. Some friends of hers were having a party in the Village, and we would take a look at it after dinner, stay if it pleased us, leave if it didn't.

Again we climbed her stairs. She took her key out but she didn't need it. The lock was intact, but the door frame was splintered. She pushed the door open, found the lights and gave a cry of dismay. I pulled her back and made a quick search to be certain we weren't interrupting anybody at his work. The apartment had been carefully, thoroughly searched. Every drawer had been dumped, every cupboard emptied. She trotted about, giving little yelps of anger, dismay and indignation. From what I could see, there was no vandalism. I grabbed her as she went by and shook her.

"Hey! Let me go!"

"Settle down. Check the valuables." She hurried into the bedroom. I followed her. All the drawers had been pulled out of the bureau, which was pulled away from the wall. She sat on the floor and began pawing through the heap of possessions. I put the drawers back in and pushed the bureau back against the wall. She found her red leather jewel-case and opened it. She went through it hastily.

She stared up at me and said, "Everything's here!"

"Are you sure?"

"Sure I'm sure. This is a solid-gold chain. Feel how heavy it is. It's worth two hundred dollars anyway . . ." She gasped suddenly and ran into the tiny kitchen. Everything was scrambled. She scuffled around and found an envelope and looked into it and said, "Oh, damn! This is gone."

"What was it?"

"Something over two hundred dollars. Maybe about two-fifty. I was putting five dollar bills in it, and when there were enough, I was going to buy a mink cape sort of thing. Damn!"

I made her check very carefully. She was so mad she wasn't very rational, but at last it was evident to both of us that the only thing taken was the money. The upholstered chairs had been tipped over, and the burlap ripped away from the springs. I put a chair on its legs and made her sit down and stop dithering. I examined the job with a reasonable amount of acquired competence. One learns by doing.

"Now hush a minute, Nina. It's no trick downstairs. You ring buzzers until somebody clicks the front door open. This door was no problem." I took a close look at the way it was broken. "Somebody worked a little pry-bar into it and slowly crunched it open. It was fast and it was thorough, Nina."

"This is *my* place," she said fiercely. "Nobody has any right . . ."

"We've got a problem," I said.

"Nobody has any right to . . . What? *We've* got a problem?"

"Somebody is either stupid or they don't give a damn."

"What?"

"Normal burglary, they'd just hit the places where people keep valuables. Bedroom drawers, desk drawers, kitchen cupboards, closet shelves. They wouldn't upend your couch and yank the burlap loose. They were after that ten thousand."

"Over two months later?"

"Think of some other answer. They came across a little bit of cash and took that. Why not? Like finding a dime on the sidewalk. If they wanted to make it look as if you were being cleaned out by a standard burglar, they would have taken your few hundred dollars worth of jewelry, your camera, your little radio, and put them in a trash can if they didn't want to risk handling them. If Plummer never left the ten thousand here, this would be a big fat mystery. And if you hadn't given it to me it would be gone now, and maybe with a hell of a lot less evidence of search around here. He would have hit the obvious places first."

"What makes you so sure of all this?"

"I'm not. I'm just trying to make sense out of it. I can take it a little further, too."

"Yes?"

"As you say, over two months have gone by. Somebody knew Plummer had that ten thousand. His sister closing his apartment could have come across it and said nothing. That would be the normal reaction of most people. So whoever did this would have to have some good reason to assume the sister didn't have it, didn't take it back to California. Maybe his place was checked before she arrived."

"Like what they did here? I didn't hear anything like that."

"What shape were you in?"

She closed her eyes for a moment. "Lost. Utterly lost, Trav."

"Who would know?"

She stirred out of the memory of grief. "Danny. Danny Gryson. He was a rock."

She made a phone call. She caught him just as he was going out. She talked to him for several minutes, with sad overtones in her voice, hidden laments in a minor key. I fixed drinks for us. When she hung up she looked at me, bit her lip, tilted her head. "I better stop criticising your guesswork, dear. Somebody got into Howie's place that Sunday and tore it all up. He couldn't see that anything in particular was missing. He just had time to put it back in shape before he had to go out to the airport and meet Grace. Danny's wife, Sally, was staying here with me, and by then I was loaded with pills. He didn't report it."

"That was damn foolish. Couldn't he see there might be a connection between that and Plummer being killed?"

"But Howie was mugged. And nobody knew anything about any money. And there was so much going on anyway."

I put the couch back on its legs and sat down. "Something doesn't fit, Nina. Something doesn't fit worth a damn."

"How, dear?"

"Plummer was threatening to upset a very big applecart. Millions. Assume he was taken out of the picture very cleverly. Why should very clever people who are stealing millions bitch up their own scheme by searching his apartment the very next day?"

"Maybe they thought he'd written up how it was being done or something and they were looking for that."

"Then why did somebody plunder this place two months later? No, honey. I think this is promising. I think we have a situation where control at the top is not too solid. The people running this are not going to give much of a damn about ten thousand dollars. But to one of the little people who are in on it, it could be a very tidy amount."

"Or somebody who was in it with Howie," she said in a small strained voice. I looked at her and saw the look of tears on the way.

"Come off it, Nina."

51

"I'm sorry. It's just that sometimes I . . ."

"Let's get to work."

It took a long time. She had a dime-store hammer and some brads. I did some temporary repairs on the door latch. I thumbtacked the burlap back on the undersides of the upholstered furniture. Once she had the kitchen back together, she laid out the rest of the things I had brought from the delicatessen. It was a buffet picnic while we brought order out of total chaos. She put records on. Folk music from Greece. Never-on-Sunday music. Most pleasant. Drinks and small spiced sturdy sandwiches and music and cooperative chores.

I waited for something to occur to her. I was stacking her books back on her shelves and she came into the living room and said, "Hey, we shouldn't get it looking too much better than it did before, Trav. That would be a terrible commentary on my . . ." She stopped and I looked at her. She was frowning.

"Trav?"

"Yes, dear."

"Aren't we going to report this to the police?"

"No."

"But if I didn't know anything about any ten thousand dollars, wouldn't I report it to the police? I mean, it would be the natural thing to do."

"Yes, it would."

"So won't whoever searched this place wonder about whether I report it or not?"

"Probably."

"And if I don't, won't he think that's because I *do* know something about the ten thousand dollars?"

"It might work that way."

She sat on a stool nearby and held her clenched hands in her lap and looked at me with her dark brows raised. "What are you trying to do? Turn me into bait?"

"On a very small chance, yes. It took him two months to come looking. Maybe you'd have spent the hell out of it by now. And anyway, we can still report it. Leave a few drawers messed up."

She nibbled at the edge of her thumb. "But it might make things happen faster if we don't?"

"There's that small chance. And I'm not going to let anything happen to you, Nina."

She stood up. "So okay. Anyhow, nothing would happen, I mean about getting my mink money back. Lois downstairs,

52

they really cleaned her out a year ago. Some of the furniture even. She was on her vacation."

She shrugged, turned in a slow circle of Greek dance, popping her fingers, and twirled on off into the bedroom. In a little while I went in and hauled the spilled mattress back up onto the bed. She finished a sandwich, licked her fingers, tried to give me a big wicked wink. But she wasn't a good winker. She couldn't close one without nearly closing the other. It made her look squinty and nearsighted.

When we had to pass in a narrow space, doing the chores of reassembling the place, she contrived to bump me with a round hip. She hummed with the music. She looked bemused and tricky and smug, darting her blue and challenging glances. When she would come to show me where something went, she would manage to press the heat of a mellow breast against my arm. She built the big awareness of girl. We were in the girl house, perfumed with girl, with blue eyes everywhere. The infrequent small-talk bore no relation to what was going on, to what she was causing.

Finally she managed to trip and turn, and be caught just so, gasping, a silky weight, breath warm, eyes knowing, lips gone soft and an inch away, and not enough air in the room.

I straightened her back up and gave her a little push. "Now, Nina, damn it, just one goddam minute, damn it!"

"Oh boy," she said. "Ethics and everything. The little sister. You talk so many bold games, it gets confusing for a girl. I guess you think it would be a lousy thing to come here to take care of me, and then take care of me too many ways, huh? But there are all kinds of lousy things. How lousy is it you should be so stuffy you make me seem sort of cheap and obvious?"

"Don't get sore."

"I'm getting mad to keep from crying. I mean you're so stuck on this role you have to play. My God, I suppose I am the little sister, but I am also an adult, Trav. I told you before I've run into some doors and had my share of black eyes. I had a disaster marriage and a very very fast annulment. But you have some kind of a boy scout oath with my brother, and . . . Now I feel degraded and . . . Damn it, get *out* of here!"

I laughed and caught her. She yawped and leaped about, saying in effect that the precious moment had passed, and the hell with it, and we couldn't retrieve the situation, it was spoiled etc etc. I stilled her mouth and each time she talked it was with a little less conviction, and finally she stood docile, trembling, taking huge noisy inhalations, her strong pale neck bent forward while, with clumsy fingers, I unlatched the little hook and eye at the back of her dress and stripped the zipper down. "This is n-n-nutty," she whispered. I told her that indeed it was. I made a silent excuse to Big Brother. I told him to give me credit for trying.

And then there was the sweet drugging time of resting, all unwound, all mysteries known, somnolent there in a narrow wedge of light from a bathroom door open a few inches. Time moves slowly then, as in an underwater world. She had hitched herself to rest upon me, so distributed that she seemed to have no weight at all. She had her dark head tucked under the angle of my jaw, her hands under me and hooked back over the tops of my shoulders, her deep breasts flattened against me, used loins resting astraddle my right thigh, a spent mild whiskery weight.

From time to time she would take a deep breath, and let it out with little catchings, little pulsings of heat against my throat. With my eyes closed, I slowly and lightly stroked the smooth contours of her back, from the moist warmth of shoulders, down to the papery coolness of the small of her back, the deep curve where she was as narrow as a child, then on to the swelling fruit of hips, richer to the touch than to the eye. When I brought my hand back, if I flattened it, pressed more strongly against the small of her back, it would bring on a little reflexive pulse of her hips, a small clamping of her fingers, a quicker inhalation—all fading echoes of the way it had been.

I felt a fatuous satisfaction in having done so much for her. In spite of all the physical attraction we had felt for each other, there had been the first-time awkwardness about it, the sense of being with a stranger, of learning and guessing and wondering. And it should all have been like that, all half-measures and falterings, leading to the need for mutual reassurances afterward. But suddenly it had all locked and steadied and deepened for us. She was no myth-figure of frenzies and clawings. Suddenly we had known all this together for a thousand years, and knew no strangeness in each other, and reached down to a deep, simple, powerful pace that released her time and time again until it became continuous for her, a vast lasting, a spending that seemed like forever.

"Golly, golly, golly," she said in a sighing whisper.

"Yes indeed."

"What hit me?"

"You're asking for a slightly bawdy answer, girl."

She chuckled and stretched against me like a cat. "Mmmm," she said. "I had some stage fright, you know. When you put the lights out and came back to me, I was wondering sort of what in the world was I doing here."

"Don't you know?"

She giggled. Then she said, "This is so nice. For afterward. Just holding and sweet and saying jokes. I can say anything to you. I can mention Howie. You don't mind if I mention Howie?"

"No."

"Afterward, it was kind of anxious with him. You know. Like when you have strangers to dinner, and you have to make sure after dinner that everything was all right. Nothing burned and nothing sour. And I wanted to be held afterward, but he always felt sort of wooden, as if it was something he had to do, and I felt unwelcome. You hold me as if you like holding me, darling. And, my God, I don't have to ask how it was. Not for me and not for you. My God, I don't ever have to wonder about it. If there is any more than that, they better not invent it, because people couldn't stand it."

She hitched up, shoved her black curls back, leaned on my chest and kissed the end of my nose. "Maybe you are too damn smart," she said. "Maybe it's all a bunch of darn technique or something."

"Don't start doubting anything."

She scowled down at me, her face in the reflection of the light that angled across her white shoulder. "Do you understand I'm not a bum? I definitely made up my mind to make you hustle me into bed."

"Stop feeling insecure, Nina. You're losing the glow."

"There were three boys before Howie, and one was that horrid little marriage, but each time it was forever. And with Howie too. You know I always felt it would be cheap and nasty and degrading to just . . . make love with a man without it being all set up to be forever. I mean a woman makes deals, doesn't she? We want security, so we trade the body for the deal, and the pleasure gets thrown in as a bonus. But the one time in my life I feel . . . well, lewd and reckless and maybe a little bit self-destructive, it turns out to be the very most there ever was for me, more than I knew there could be, damn it. But this wasn't just for recreation. It was more than that. I'm not a tramp. But maybe I'm not what I thought I was, either."

She settled back the way she had been, tucking her hands under me. She sighed. "Talk, talk, talk. I just never felt so . . . so unwound and undone and sweetened. Oh boy, the constant miracle of me. Bores talk endlessly about themselves. Keep patting me. I don't want to lose the glow. I don't want to go back out into the cold world. Darling, *am* I talking too much?"

"No."

"If I stopped babbling would you like to have a nap?"

"No."

She laid in thoughtful stillness for a little time, then pulled her right arm free and rested her curled fist on my chest. "I want to keep on feeling good, but I'm beginning to get scared again. In a different way. Tell me everything is all right."

"I give too many lectures."

"You have to talk to me before you turn into a stranger again, dear."

"Reassurances? What do you want of me? Do you want me to buy back your self-respect by telling you I love you?"

She stiffened. She pushed herself up quickly. She sat, facing me, hugging her legs, her canted head resting on her knees, the round of her hip fitting into my waist. "That was kind of a cruel dirty cold thing to say, Trav."

"Shock treatment."

"What the hell good does it do?"

"By feeling insecure about our making love, Nina, you make the inference we are a pair of cheap people involved in some cheap pleasant friction. Pull on the pants and walk away, adding up the score. I think we're interested in each other, involved with each other, curious about each other. This was a part of exploring and learning. When it's good you learn something about yourself too. If the spirit is involved, if there is tenderness and respect and awareness of need, that's all the morality I care about. Take your choice, honey. It's up to you. You can look at us from the inside, and we can be Nina Gibson and Travis McGee, heightened and brightened and expanded by something close and rare and dear. Or you can look at it from the outside, and then it makes you that silly little broad I banged when I was up in New York. And it turns me into playboy McGee, smirking and winking. It turns an importance into a cruddy diversion."

She closed her eyes. In the path of bathroom light her face looked small and pale and still. Her hands were clasped.

Her cheek still rested on her round knees. It is one of the lovely and classic postures of a woman.

She opened her eyes and said, "I think I can accept that, if I keep trying. But be patient. I've got a lot of cruddy old conservative traditional ideas about this kind of thing. I don't even know why I wanted to seduce you. I felt terribly wicked and reckless. If I say something now, will you promise not to take it the wrong way?"

"All right."

"I love you. And I'm not trying to buy back anything. Or claim anything. Or promote anything."

"Thank you, Nina."

She smiled. "That was the only right thing you could have said. You're welcome. Love is a gift, not a bargain. That's something to learn, I guess. But what could you have learned from me?"

"That a nineteen-inch waist is delicious."

"Please don't make jokes."

"I learned that I'm growing older."

"What do you mean by that?"

"There was a very special sweetness about you I couldn't identify, Nina. A sad, ceremonial, ritualistic sweetness. It became a kind of a love rite."

"I sensed a little of that, darling."

"And there was a strange feeling of familiarity, a haunted feeling. Now I know what made it so special, an odd little feeling that you might be my very last bitter-sweet girl, the last one I will ever know with such an unused flavor of innocence about her, an almost childish wonder and intensity. It made me feel that so much of your life is ahead of you, and I have used up so much of mine."

"Don't," she whispered. "I want you to be glad about me."

"I am. I don't go hunting for regret. Maybe when joy is a little conditional, it's sharper."

"Darling, I don't feel childish and I don't feel innocent, and God knows I'm a long long way from feeling unused. Don't patronize me. I really think of myself as grown up. I earn a hundred and sixty dollars a week. I've buried the man I was going to marry. I wasn't a whimpering little ninny, was I? I made love like a grown woman. Please don't turn me into the symbolic girl in some sad little self-involved drama of McGee. As you said, I'm Nina Gibson. I'm not typical of anything but me. Ceremony? I guess I'm glad it was ceremonious for us. But no alligator tears, darling Trav. And if this doesn't sound too insane, I think I would like

57

to go to that party. I want to put something in between us and us. I want a thinking time."

"Sure."

She uncurled and leaned and kissed me and then got up. She glanced at me. The shaft of light touched the outside of my right thigh, the ugliness of the long guttered scar—deep, puckered, banded with the white welts of shiny tissue.

She made a little whistling suck of air through her teeth, then reached and traced the length of the scar with her healing fingertips. That is the test of a total woman. The squeamish ones shy away with sick face. They are the half women, the cringing delicate ones, who are never worth a damn in bed. A complete woman, more than any man could ever be, is involved in the realities, the elemental dynamics of life, the blood and pain and mess of it, cleaning and healing. In this is all the enduring lustiness of their purposes and their needs. "They hurt you," she said. This, too, is one of the elemental statements of life.

"I used to have a romantic limp."

"I shouldn't wonder."

"It got infected, and I wasn't in a situation where I could get it treated."

"Why not?"

"Some people were looking for me."

"You could have lost your leg."

"They told me that, too."

It was a big loft-apartment, hung with masks and action paintings, loud with chatter and Haitian beat, with meager lights, a sparce collection of junk furniture, scores of soiled pillows, forty or more guests. I found a place to stand, a wall to lean upon, a drink to hold. Half the guests, like Nina, had the little apologetic flavor of success of those who have moved uptown. The others had that boisterous defensive arrogance of the *in* group, with cryptic talk and compulsive disdain. Nothing had changed since I had last attended a party in that area, some four years before. I could identify the types—the fierce, sad, bearded young men and their bra-less girls in ballet shoes, the Petulant Fairy, the Orgiastic Dancer, the Symbolic Negro, the Brave Couples, the Jealous Dike, Next Year's Playwright, the Girl who would Throw-Up-Later-On, the Symbolic Communist, the Traditional Nymphomaniac, the Eager Tourist and the Wise Old Sculptor with Bad Breath.

I kept seeing my Nina, always on the far side of the

room, in a dark green fuzzy-soft dress, a necklace of gold coins. I had zippered her into that dress, and made of that small ceremony a delaying game that nearly canceled our attendance. Whenever I met her blue glance across the room, we were as alone as if none of the others existed.

People kept drifting up and digging at me to see what manner of animal this might be. A bone-thin blonde with a big bite mark on her sallow neck came and leaned loosely upon me and said, "Cruddy bottles and tubes and pots. She had a teenyweeny lil talent, but it was honest. Right? Where do you fit in, buster boy? You square as that other one, that investment type?"

"I'm in marine hardware," I said earnestly.

"You're in what, buster?"

"Leisure-time America has taken to the waterways. A boating America is a healthy America."

She unhooked herself and peered at me. "Oh dear Jesus," she said.

"We're launching a new line of nylon cleats in decorator colors."

She worked thin lips as though considering spitting, and then drifted away, scratching herself.

A round young man with blond bangs explained how he and a darling friend of his would each write exactly five pages of description of the same sexual experience, using the same typewriter and the same spacing, and then they would cut the pages in half, vertically, and paste them together, so that the left half of each page was written by a different person than the one who wrote the right half. Then a third darling friend would retype the ten-page manuscript, sticking in any bridge words that struck his fancy.

"It's the duality of it that makes it so magical," he said. "It's truly a complex of our images. Charles thinks we should publish, now that we have fifteen of them. We're selling shares at fifty dollars."

"I'm in marine hardware," I said.

"Oh?"

"Maybe you could try that system to write us some copy on our new imitation-teak decking."

"Surely you jest."

"You could check it out with the agency. They use some way-out stuff sometimes. You know. Like Picasso. Those guys."

"Like Picasso," he said faintly. "Those guys." He tottered off, fingering his bangs.

I met a few nice ones, Nina's special friends, a girl with good and steady eyes, and a wry and likeable man who worked for a publishing house. They were properly protective of her, looking me over with great care, giving a dubious approval. I stalked Nina into a corner and said, "Had enough of this?"

"Let's see if we can last ten more horrible minutes."

"Five," I said, looking into blue, down into blue, teetering on the edge of blue depths.

She bit her lips and eyes widened. "Three," she said.

"Minutes or seconds?"

"Find my coat and I'll go say goodby for us."

So we rolled home in taxi-laughter and climbed the stairs, and with slow and loving care and myriad interruptions, I undressed her into the rowdy bed. We gamboled and romped like love-struck kids until we sobered into our ultimate ceremony and this time she called to me. "Trav, Trav, Trav-isssss!" It was a night of small entangled sleeps and awakenings. Our uses seemed to deepen the hunger rather than blunt or diminish it. We became more violently sensitized to each other, more skilled and knowing in the plunder. It is a rare thing, that infatuation which grows with each sating, so that those caresses which are merely affection and the gratitude of release and sleepy habit turn in their own slow time into the next overture, the next threshold, the next unwearied increment of heat and need, using and knowing, learning and giving, new signs and signals in a private and special language, freshened heats and scents and tastes, sweetened gasps of fitting thus, knowing this, learning of that, rediscovering the inexhaustible here, the remorseless now.

In an early sunlight of Sunday I dressed slowly. She lay foundered and pungent in the turmoiled bed, deep in her honeyed sleep. When I was ready to go, I sat on the edge of the bed and kissed her salty temple and a smudged eyelid. She murmured and slowly raised a hundredweight of head and peered at me from a small sleep-sodden face. Then she lunged and hung soft arms around my neck, sagging heavily against me, and mumbled, "Doan go way."

"I'll be back."

"Um."

"You get some sleep, darling."

"Uh huh."

I kissed her and caressed her, and she began to stir at once into her sensitized response. I laughed and unlocked her arms and laid her back down. I covered her up, tucked her

60

in, patted the high round mound of her hip. She murmured and was immediately asleep. I fixed the blinds to darken the room, and left her there.

I decided to walk until I found a cruising cab, but after two blocks decided to walk all the way. There was a rasp of beard on my jaws and my eyes felt sandy. There is an odd feeling some would call the post-coital depression. I felt drab, as if my muscles were no longer firmly affixed to the bone, as if the bone itself had become leaden and weighty. Such a hunger, such a using-up, seemed part of a pattern of betrayal. Betrayal of the blinded brother, and of a dead man I had never known, and of the girl herself. Perhaps that was the reason for sadness, the awareness of a merciless using. I had been strongly attracted by the strange freshness of her, her flavor of being unused, a kind of clear-eyed innocence. Virginity is a very relative term. Walking the empty streets I convinced myself that I had thoroughly eroded the very thing which had attracted me. It was a mournful and romantic concept. She had the look of a girl who had never spent such a night as the one just past. And her body had all the tastes and flavors of discovery. Every weary lover can, with just a little trouble, turn himself into an insufferable horse's ass. I had the impertinence to mourn my Nina's loss of innocence. Conventional McGee, guilty debaucher of girls. I fancied that when she awoke, when she remembered all, she might feel appalled and stricken by too many rude and undignified uses, efforts which by light of day she would think grotesque. The wearied lover becomes very stately and very indignant at himself. He is a Tory, despising his own bacchanal.

When I got up to my room the red light on my phone was blinking. The operator told me that Mrs. Drummond had called me several times, and that her last message was to return her call whenever I got back. It was twenty after eight.

The same maid I had talked to before answered the phone. A Gabor accent. I wondered if that was some kind of typecasting. She had me wait. I waited five minutes.

Terry Drummond barked into the phone. "Tomcatting, were you? Are you sober, sweetie?"

"Completely."

"The office pig is joining me for brunch, here at the hotel."

"What about Connecticut?"

"This is more interesting. Is there any chance she might know you or know anything about you?"

"No."

"Good. She is meeting me at one. I want you to arrive at two-thirty. To meet me. I'll tell her I'm expecting you. Then I shall make a horrible scene after you get there. Just follow my lead, sweetie. I am going to be a sickening bitch. It's a character bit I'm used to. Then I shall sweep out and leave you with the pig. I'll give her a bit of a going-over too, so then you'll be fellow victims."

"What good does that do?"

"Are you certain you aren't drunk, sweetie? When we talked, you seemed like quite a clever shifty fellow. And terribly attractive in a sort of brown brutal way. You must be enormously successful with shop girls and such. Why should the office pig be less vulnerable? Cozy up to her, sweetie. You would be a nice change for her, after poor Charlie. And we do want to find out what the hell is going on, don't we? Just bat those terrible pale gray eyes at her, and show your white teeth and bulge your muscles a little. She'll go all weak in the knees."

"Oh, naturally."

"Well . . . didn't I?"

"You have notoriously weak knees, Terry."

"You're *such* a bastard. See you here at two-thirty."

I undressed. I showered long, rinsing away the subtle pungencies of love, hung out my do-not-disturb sign, left a call and toppled into bed.

seven

MY PHONE woke me a few minutes before my twelve-thirty call.

I answered it and Nina said, "Well?"

"Oh. Hi, darling."

"You have a girl over here. Remember?"

"What's your name again?"

"My name is I love you McGee."

"You sound pretty merry."

"I feel absolutely stupendous. I have deep black circles under my eyes, and I have this uncontrollable twitch, and I limp on both hind legs, and I never felt better in my life. And I miss you. Terribly. What have you been doing? Sleeping? What's the matter with you? No stamina?"

"When did you wake up?"

"Five minutes ago. And I'm about to take a great big steaming hot bath and wash my hair."

I told her about Terry's call, but I did not tell her Terry's suggestion about Bonita Hersch.

She was disappointed. I said I would make it just as soon as I could.

I paused at the entrance and looked into the brunch area. A lot of the tables had emptied. They were at a table on the right, over at the side. Terry spotted me and waved. She wore a casual tweed suit, a small brown hat, and looked smart and very much at ease. As I walked toward the table I looked at the other woman. There was a stiffness in her posture. She wore a black dress. Her fur was over the back of her chair. She wore a rather intricate hat atop a careful sculpturing of pumpkin-gold hair. From a distance she bore a rather striking resemblance to Princess Grace Kelly Ranier. But as I neared the table I saw there was a coarseness in

63

her face, features slightly heavier. She looked to be about thirty.

A waiter quickly moved a chair to the table. "Hello, darling," Terry cawed. "Bonita dear, this is Travis McGee, Trav, Miss Bonita Hersch. You're a few minutes late, darling."

"Sorry."

Her smile was wicked. "You're not too terribly attentive, dear. I'd hate to think that I bore you."

"You couldn't bore me, Terry," I said, and asked the waiter to bring me some coffee.

"Isn't he decorative, Bonita? Look at those monstrous shoulders. But he's really frightfully proper and dull and just a little bit stupid."

"Take it easy, Terry."

"My God, is that a command? Aren't we masterful today? Perhaps you bore me."

"Come off it, Terry, for God's sake."

"Am I embarrassing you, Trav? Gracious! Isn't it odd how the friends of one's friends never quite work out? Next time I see Bunny I shall tell her that you certainly lived up to the advance billing, but by the cold light of day, you depress me." She gathered her purse and cigarettes and stood up looking at us with seamed monkey-smile. I got slowly to my feet.

"Oh, stay right here, dear. Wait for your coffee and have a nice little chat with Bonita. You and she should get along marvelously. She's a dreary little typist who seems to think she's going to marry my sister's husband, poor thing. She's rather sexy in a crude way, don't you think? Have a charming time, dears."

She went swiftly away, smiling at friends, her stride vital and youthful.

"She is a terrible, terrible woman," Bonita said in an awed and trembling voice. "Nobody has ever talked to me like that before."

I took a more careful look at Bonita Hersch. Her grooming was almost too perfect. Every little golden hair was in place. Her eyes were a pale cold gray-blue. Under the disguise of lipstick, her upper lip was very thin and her under lip was full and heavy. Her hands were wide and rather plump, with short thick fingers.

"She was very rude to you, Miss Hersch."

"She invited me here."

"That makes it unforgivable."

"It certainly does. And she got everything wrong. Things

64

aren't at all . . . the way she said they are. Do you know her well?"

"Not very well. Somebody asked me to look her up. She's a spoiled woman, Miss Hersch."

"I am not going to try to understand why she was rude." There was a little more edge and authority in her voice, but it was a light-bodied voice. It had a hushed and confidential quality about it.

"Let's try to forget Terry Drummond. I don't have to have that coffee. Maybe we could go somewhere else and I could buy you a drink?"

She turned those appraising eyes on me. A sharp pink tongue-tip was momentarily visible at the corner of her mouth. She looked at a small jeweled watch, lifting the ornamental cap with the edge of her thumb nail. "I think that would be very nice, Mr. McGee."

"Fine," I said. I stood up and took her chair. She stood up and moved away from the table and waited for me to hang her fur wrap on her shoulders. She had a long slender back. Her breasts were small and high. The black dress was exquisitely fitted to her, particularly effective in displaying the long ripe lines of her heavy and elegant and firmly-girdled hips. She smiled formal thanks, with a little flicker of darkened eyelashes over her shoulder at me, and then walked out ahead of me, walking with that very slight awkwardness, more illusion than reality, of long-waisted women sensuously and consciously overripe in hip and thigh. At each short stride the calves of her legs swelled round and smooth under sheer nylon, making her ankles look more fragile than they were.

She settled into the cab, in a spiced fragrance of her perfume and smiled and said, "If I might choose . . ."

"Of course."

"Driver, Armitage Inn, please. Lexington at Fif . . ."

"I know where it is, lady."

"As you interrupted me, driver, I was about to tell you to go to the side entrance." There was a little silken whip in that voice, and it made a nice little pop when she got her wrist into it.

Her morale was improving. I saw what was wrong about her. She was just too bloody refeened.

"Do you live in the city, Mr. McGee?"

"Florida, Miss Hersch."

"Can we be . . . what did she call you. Trav? Trav and Bonita? I must warn you. Please do not call me Bonny.

65

I wondered abour your marvelous tan, Trav. Are you in business in Florida?"

"I'm a boat-bum, Bonita."

"Oh?" I detected a faint chill.

"I have a custom houseboat down there. I live aboard. I get into a few little things now and then, but mostly I do as little as possible."

"It sounds like a lovely life." The chill was gone.

I could realize how bright Terry had been. She had put Bonita Hersch in such a bad light that the woman would feel obligated to correct the picture. And she had given me, by indirection, the sort of credentials which would make me seem both interesting and harmless to Bonita.

I had to admire her choice of a place. We were given a deep red-leather booth with sides high enough to assure privacy. There was inoffensive background music, lighting designed to make women lovelier, and excellent service.

She shook her head sadly. "That woman. What did she call me? A dreary typist. Now it seems amusing. I do type. Once upon a time I was a typist. But I've never felt particularly dreary. I'm an executive secretary—private secretary to Charles McKewn Armister. And I certainly do not care to marry anyone. Then I *would* feel dreary. Do you know, that implausible woman offered me a huge sum of money to send Mr. Armister back to his wife? She couldn't be more mistaken, really."

"What gave her the idea you could?"

"She misinterpreted a certain situation, Trav. In a way I can't blame her for that. I imagine a great many people have the same idea. But she could have listened to an explanation. You see, I live in Mr. Armister's apartment. But so does Mr. Baynard Mulligan, his personal attorney and the head of his legal staff. And a chauffeur. And a cook. It's quite large. There are five bedrooms and four baths in addition to the servants' quarters. I worked for Mr. Mulligan for several years. When Mr. Armister's secretary retired a year ago, I replaced her, at Mr. Mulligan's suggestion and with Mr. Armister's approval. I'm perfectly willing to admit that it is a strange arrangement, but I function as a housekeeper, in a sense. I run the staff and supervise the buying and the menu—that sort of thing. They are both very busy men. It's a convenience for them. It costs me very little to live these days, but I must admit that I hated giving up my own little place. I'm actually starved for privacy, Trav. I would have loved to have had you see my precious little apartment."

"Then there never was anything between you and Charlie Armister?"

I was again aware of her calculating appraisal. "Nothing important or enduring. Just a little time of foolishness. It ended months ago. Proximity, I suppose. It can be so dangerous, you know. And Charlie is a dear, dear man. He made me forget one of my basic rules of behavior. A girl should never never never have an affair with the man she works for. It's such a stupid thing to do. It always has to end, you know, and then there's the terrible awkwardness of trying to work smoothly together, and usually the man gets rid of the secretary somehow. And it might mean a much less important job. I've seen that kind of thing happen far too often. So I've made it a rule. It seems Charlie was the exception. But we survived it nicely, without impairing the working relationship."

"That was fortunate."

"Yes indeed it was. I have a tremendous capacity for loyalty, Trav. I give the man I work for all my energy and competence. That's what I'm paid to do, to increase his working efficiency, protect him, advise him when he asks. There has to be . . . a rather formal flavor about it to make it work. Do you understand?"

"I think so."

"Any wise and ambitious woman will compartment her office life and her private life. I imagine Mrs. Drummond heard some rumor or other, and she must think it is still going on. But it isn't, of course. She could just as well try to bribe Martha, our German cook, to send Charlie back to Joanna."

"That marriage is on the rocks?"

"Apparently. He was terribly repressed, and now he's broken out and I don't believe he'll ever want to go back to the kind of life he led before. He's really a very happy man now."

"Is he going with anyone?"

"Trav! Remember what I said about loyalty? I really can't discuss the man I work for, can I?"

I swallowed the temptation to ask her what she had been doing. I smiled at her, thinking that this was as nasty a bit as I had come across in a long time. I could sense the ruthless pursuit of the career. And her equivalently ruthless pursuit of sexual gratification. This was the product of a dozen highly competitive offices, of skilled infighting, merciless intrigue.

Her heart was as cold as a stone at the bottom of a mountain lake.

Her bosses would remember her as a jewel. Her lovers would remember her as an enchanting mistress. She would embody all the cheap glamour techniques, the skillful arrangements of Sex-and-the-Single-Girl. She would pick her lovers the way an IBM sorter finds a new sales manager. Married men would suit her best. They weren't as likely to be a nuisance, create scenes and difficulties. I saw a succession of dapper and slightly puffy fellows with little black mustaches, gold bill-clips, hard-top convertibles and small stock options. They would all say Bonita is a good sport. Bonita knows how to make a man feel like a king. There were no hard feelings. We're-still-good-friends. Very clever girl. Fastidious.

A precious little apartment and sexy hostess pyjamas, candlelight and little taste-treats cooked in shiny copper pots. Mild music and deft little conversational bits, and then after she had stacked the pots and dishes for her precious little maid to take care of the next day, she would delicately bower herself in silk and perfume, all coiffed and tidily diaphragmed, with the lights just so, and pull the poor dazzled son-of-a-bitch, marveling at his luck, onto those deep soft hungry cannibal loins. Because when a girl does without, she gets a little edgy, and lots of authorities say it is sort of a beauty therapy, my dear, keeping the glands in order and all. It's good for the skin.

But if poor Harry the Mustache happened to work for the same outfit, and happened to get in her way or the way of her boss, she could open his throat with the same indifferent skill with which she had learned to cut radishes into precious little rosettes. And when one Harry would become too accustomed to her, and begin to take all that stylized graciousness for granted, with too little humble gratitude, she would skilfully shuck him and begin her patient search for the next one. From each she would absorb some special field of knowledge—wines or paintings, sports cars or antique glass—because she wants so terribly to become truly and totally refeened.

This was a guileful, perfumed monster. God only knows where they come from. They clump up in the big cities. Somehow they all manage to look quite a lot like each other. They consider themselves sophisticates. They buy growth stocks. They worry a lot about their breasts and about secretarial spread. The idea of ever having a baby is some kind

68

of a grotesque joke. It would hurt. And then you'd be stuck with it. Their conversation is fantastically up to date. They get the very best of service everywhere they go. And when, at last, they begin to get a little scared, they go on the biggest and most careful hunt of all. The big game they are after has a triple listing—D and B, Social Register and Who's Who. And with all their polished skills, they wrench the poor bastard away from his wife, nail him, and—in smug luxury— ruin all the years he has left.

Her smile was practiced and charming. Her makeup, hair styling and dress design were carefully planned to enhance every good feature.

"Trav, dear, let's drink to dreary rich women like poor Terry. And to Sunday afternoons in October. And to finding new friends."

"And to privacy."

She made a rueful face. "That lovely thing which I ain't got. I really have to be alone a little while every day. It renews me, you know? I pity people who haven't enough resources to be able to be by themselves. In that huge apartment, I lock myself in my room and think and read. I read a great deal. It's the only way we have to lead more lives than one."

"That's a very interesting way of putting it, Bonita."

She arranged her face into a pretty little frown of thought. "I suppose we all feel trapped in one life. Sometimes it makes one want to do mad mad things. It's dreary to be circumspect *all* the time."

"Think up a madness."

"Sure," she said. She made her cold eyes sparkle. "Take a cab right now, to Idlewild. Buy a toothbrush, fly to Florida, and go off on your boat and hide away in the islands."

"I'll go check the flights."

"Darling, I do wish I could. I really do. But sometimes we all have to settle for a little less, don't we?"

It was a very personal voice. It was good for nuances. She was beginning to make me feel like a juicy bug on the end of a handy twig. Any minute now the sticky tongue would flick out and snare me and yank me into that greedy maw. She was managing it with great skill. She had fed me most of my lines.

"What will you settle for, Bonita?"

"Another drink, dear."

"That's a very minor request."

69

"Everything is relative, Trav. Everything should be sufficient to the moment, don't you think?"

"It seldom is."

"That's because most people never know exactly what they want. It's a great blessing, to always know exactly what you want."

"Do you?"

"You still didn't order that drink."

After I did, she said, "Will you be in town long?"

"Another few days. A week. Maybe a little more."

"Are you staying with friends?" I named my hotel. She looked disapproving. "Those new ones are so characterless."

"And completely anonymous. I like that kind of privacy."

"Are the rooms really nice? I picture them as little white boxes."

"They're quite comfortable."

She glanced down for a fraction of a second, and I knew that she had opened that jeweled watch. Her lips tightened slightly. I was being a dull pupil. I wondered if she'd take me by the ear and lead me, bellowing, back to my hotel room. She had the hunger, she had set the scene, and she was pressed for time. But I had suddenly forgotten my lines.

I saw her begin to wonder if I found her unattractive. The thought disturbed her. I had to take her off the hook. "I wish I could see that apartment you used to have."

"But I had to give it up, dear. It broke my heart. All my precious things in storage. And I can't show you the apartment where I live now. I'm . . . not really in a position to have guests. Surely you understand."

"Of course, Bonita." I was beginning to have a difficult time relating her to conspiracy, to large-scale theft, to possible murder. She was clear-eyed and healthy. The long round pale throat had a look of grace and strength. She was fragrant and purposeful, and she knew how to use her eyes and mouth to maximum effect. She sat there, humid and intent, leaning slightly forward, with a tilted smile, planted firmly on those glossy needful hips, readied for any opportunity to rationalize a brief Sunday-afternoon liaison as a bit of enchanting October madness, concealing with a hasty jerry-built scaffolding of romance the plain vulgar structure of itch. Her living arrangement had deprived her, apparently, and though she was more accustomed to the leisurely pursuits fashioned about the precious little apartment, she was obviously willing to gratify herself in a more casual fashion when opportunity arose. And, because of Terry, I had a suitable cachet. Once a reasonably attractive woman has accustomed herself to an almost masculine directness, her batting average can run unreasonably high. And such was her skill she had injected a thoroughly steamy overtone into the conversation without ever having committed herself in any way. Were I to dutifully trundle her off to the gold and white lobby and up to my plastic aerie, she would arrange to get herself kissed, then laugh fondly and patronizingly and chide me for being a dear silly boy, then put her black dress on a hanger and carefully turban her intricate hair with a towel to keep it from being mussed, and graciously, generously, coyly present herself for service, giving her explicit executive-secretarial instructions and requests in that light-bodied, musical, secretive voice. October madness, my dear. Everything sufficient to the moment. We all have to settle for what we can get. Eased and content, she would dress with great care, making a gay chatter all the while, and, at the door, pat my cheek fondly and call me a dear boy, quite confident I would never never forget this magical afternoon when a veritable princess had brightened my drab days with her impulsive generosity.

Playing it her way, a game for which I had no stomach, would end the relationship. Offending her would end it just as readily. If I were to learn anything from her, I had to achieve some kind of continuity.

"Bonita, I could prove that the rooms are not little white boxes, but I think Walker might wake up in a bad temper."

"Walker?"

"He was a little too tight to drive back to the country last night. Bunny's nephew."

"Oh?"

"Bunny Rodriguez. Terry mentioned her."

"Oh, yes, of course," she said with a little uncertain frown between her golden brows.

"When I left to meet Terry, he didn't look as if he would wake up until Monday." I smiled at her. "There's an old phrase: Had I but known."

She reached swiftly and patted my hand. "Tours of inspection are dull things at best, my dear. And we certainly don't want to disturb Walker, do we?"

"I could have him evicted."

"You're fun, Trav. I do like being with you."

"A pair of refugees from Terry Drummond. I suppose it's the money. People with that kind of money are never

71

quite real. I can't imagine Charles McKewn Armister as being quite real, Bonita."

"Oh he is, definitely. But he does have some unreal attitudes, I suppose. I remember while I was still working for Bay. That was well over a year ago, before Charles became ill. Charles came back from having lunch at one of his clubs one day, and he was very indignant. He was used to paying a dollar and a half for his lunch, and they had raised the price to a dollar sixty-five. He wrote an indignant letter to the house committee. I suppose he had lunch there twenty times a year. Twenty times fifteen cents comes to three dollars. And it was that same month that he and his wife gave seven hundred thousand dollars to Princeton. Out of foundation monies of course. But the contrast."

"Terry said he doesn't use his clubs any more."

There was a cold flicker in her pale blue eyes. "Not lately. You see, they are making huge changes in the investment setup of the Armister money. And when Charlie goes out, even if he went to a private club, there are just too many people who are too anxious to find out what the plans are, and suggest things and try to gain some advantage. After all, when you start moving some seventy millions of dollars about, people get some terribly clever ideas. It's part of my job to . . . to insulate Charlie from those people." She patted my hand again, more lingeringly. "But I don't want to talk shop, dear. This is a rare day off for me. It's practically a vacation. I should be back at the apartment by seven at the latest."

"And here it is quarter to four. Will I be able to see you soon again, Bonita?"

She looked rueful. "It's really terribly difficult, Trav. I'm at their beck and call."

"Aren't your evenings your own?"

"They should be. But it hasn't worked out that way. I do special work at the apartment for Baynard. One of the extra bedrooms is set up as an office now. This is a very busy time for all of us. But . . . you could give me a ring. At the office would be best."

I ordered us another round. The drinks were getting to her slightly, but they did not make her any less evasive when I tried to swing the conversation around to Charlie Armister.

Finally I said, "How much did Terry offer you to send Charlie back to Joanna?"

She bit her lip. "I suppose Terry would tell you anyway. Fifty thousand dollars. Isn't that absurd?"

I shrugged. "She's got it. And she loves her sister. Too bad you couldn't send him back."

"Charlie is a generous employer."

"Not that generous, is he?"

"No. But I have more than enough for my needs, Trav."

"Your expensive tastes?"

She smiled. "Clothes and furs. And nice surroundings. But if I had millions, I think I'd keep working. It's my life."

"Power hungry?"

"It's my weakness, dear. I love to have the little people jump when I want them to jump. I have an earnest little secretary of my own. Miss Angela Morse. She's a fat humble little thing, and she strives so hard to please. She gets all sweaty when I speak to her. But in a few years I might be able to really turn her into something."

I filed that away. A little later I was able to take another hack at Charlie-lore. She left a small opening and I said, "When he had his nervous breakdown, did he come right back and move into the apartment?"

"What nervous breakdown, dear?"

"All right. When he was sick."

"Yes, he wanted to stay in town. Baynard found the apartment. We moved in and got it all ready for him. He was very pleased with it."

"And then you and he had your little fling."

"Darling, you're going to make me terribly sorry I ever mentioned that. He couldn't spend much time at the office. I took things back for his signature and so on. And, as I said, it was proximity. Terry acted as if I were some horrible little slut trying to snag myself a rich man. I have more pride than that."

"That's obvious."

"Why do we keep talking about Charlie?"

"Maybe I'm jealous."

She took hold of my wrist, a firm pressure in her small plump hand. "You shouldn't be, dearie. It's been over for months. And I have been a veritable nun ever since."

"And Charlie has been a monk?"

"Hardly!"

"You sound very positive."

"Didn't I tell you he's recovering from a life of repression? He has whole acres of wild oats all saved up. So poor Baynard, to keep Charlie from making a fool of himself, or to keep some bitch from blackmailing him, has been . . . well, arranging things for him."

73

"Ladies of the evening?"

"It distresses poor Baynard. But from what little I have seen of a couple of them, they seem quite presentable. I guess if you pay enough they would be. They look like college girls who do some modeling on the side. I don't know what the source is, but apparently it's inexhaustible. Harris goes and picks them up in the Lincoln and brings them up the service elevator. They leave in the morning the same way. I imagine they are perfectly trustworthy. And it does keep him out of trouble. It seems so strange that . . ." She stopped abruptly and released my wrist. She stared at me. "I must be getting drunk, Trav. I shouldn't be saying these things."

"You're among friends."

She drew herself up. "Am I? Perhaps you're pumping me. How do I know that Terry Drummond didn't arrange this so you could pump me, dear?"

"You're getting to be paranoid."

"Hardly. I'm just naturally cautious. And very loyal. I told you how loyal I am. I am very very loyal to the man I work for. And I am very very loving to the man I *don't* work for."

"Baynard?"

"Don't be a dope. I meant it abstract."

"But you are a nun, you said."

"Yes indeed. Tragic, isn't it? But that's the way the ball bounces sometimes. Did I ask for this drink? How many does this make? Is it sinful to get smashed on Sunday, dear?"

"It's the best day."

She beamed and preened herself and fluttered her eyelashes. "What a man wants, he doesn't want *involvement*. You know? I know how a man thinks. I think like a man, darling. Does that seem strange?"

"Not at all."

"A man wants to have his fun and no regrets. Fair for one, fair for all. Right?"

"Right."

"Promiskus . . . promiscuous means like cheating on a man. I've always said Bonita, you've got to be loving and loyal, because you don't want to be a tramp. Geez, I miss my darling lil apartment so much. A girl should be a good sport. You know? God, I hate a teaser. That's false pretenses. Right?"

"Right."

"A man wants you gracious. Nice lil private dinners and pretty sexy clothes. Good cooking. Herbs. I use lots of herbs. And damned good in bed. That's what counts the most, let me tell you, sonny boy." She stopped again and her eyes widened. She wore a listening expression. Suddenly there were beads of moisture on her pale forehead.

"Scuse me," she said in a tiny voice and got up quickly and hurried away, leaning forward slightly from the waist. She was gone a long time. When she came back she looked slightly hollow-eyed. But sobered.

"I think you'd better take me home, dear."

At 121 East 71st, the doorman held the door for us. I walked her past the desk and back to the elevators. She smiled her weak apologetic thanks, touched my hand and stepped in and pressed the button for the ninth floor.

I went to the desk. The pale clerk looked suspiciously at me through heavy glasses. "Yes sir?"

"Miss Hersch was feeling faint. I want to give her a chance to get up there and then phone up and see if she is all right."

He hesitated, nodded, lifted a house phone onto the counter. He plugged me into 9A and rang.

Bonita answered. "Yes?"

"Trav. I wanted to be sure you got up there all right."

"I'm all right. Sweet of you to phone."

"I'd like to see you again."

"Phone me at the office, dear. Thank you for the drinks and the nice talk."

I thanked the clerk and went out. The early dusk was arriving. There was a chill in the air. I exchanged weather pleasantries with the doorman and gave him a dollar to whistle me up a cab. I wanted him to remember me as the legitimate guest of a resident of his carefully guarded tower.

I knocked at Nina's door. She opened it, grabbed me and hauled me in. After a devoted business of kissing, I held her at arm's length to admire her. She had her hair pulled back and tied. She wore a flowered blouse and sexy black stretch-pants. She looked fresh as morning, dainty as lace, innocent as a field of lambs. She gave me a vast bawdy wink that screwed up half her face.

"It's the only way I can wink," she said. "Unless I hold the other eye shut. And that looks ridiculous. Where the hell have you been?"

"How are you for guilt and regrets?"

She looked blankly at me. "Guilt? Regrets? Heck, if I've decided not to be prim, why should you bring it up?"

"Just to be sure."

"I've invented fifty more things we can do. Darling, you're like owning the key to the candy store."

"You frighten me."

"Good! Where have you been?"

"With a female creature. Let me tell you about you. After being with her in an intimate bar, Miss Nina, you are exceptionally glorious. You are invaluable. You are honest and true."

"Of course."

"There is a very smart little male spider who first grabs a bug and wraps it up and then a-courting goes, hoping he can be done and away before the big savage female spider finishes eating the bug."

"Did you bring me a bug?"

"No."

"Pretty careless of you."

"One should take a bug to Bonita Hersch."

"Did you?"

"I didn't go near the web."

"If you ever do, McGee, I'll peel you with a dull knife and feed you to the snakes."

"You're very fierce today, Miss Gibson."

"Man, I'm plain savage. And healthy. And tired of waiting."

With no warning except a sudden expression of mischief, she leaped up at me, wrapped her arms high around my neck and locked her legs around my waist. She put her teeth into the side of my neck and made a small and comfortable snarling sound. I strolled around with her as if she weren't there. I whistled a small tune, picked up a part of her Sunday paper and looked at it, went out into the kitchen and got a drink of water. Then I wandered in and sat on her bed. She brought her head around and put her nose against mine, her eyes wide and staring.

"Nina, dear! Where did you come from?"

"Wanna play owl?"

"Certainly. How do you play?"

"Just like this. Open your eyes wide too. First one blinks is a lousy owl."

She won three straight rounds of owl. I told her that if she played my rules, she wouldn't find it so easy to win. She said she'd play anybody's rules and still win. I said my game was called naked owl. She said she would be delighted to show me I was outclassed. We stacked the clothing on a chair. I won three straight rounds. She called me a dirty sneaking cheat, and said that if all I came around for was a bunch of kid games, I could go right back to Bonita. I said that the way this game had developed, it was no longer for kids. It was more like a game for the young adult. She said that if everybody would hold still for just one cotton-picking minute, she could win the final game and break the tie, because you couldn't play any kind of a game well if your attention kept wandering.

She was a joy. She won by disconcerting me. She slowly crossed her big blue eyes and crowed with triumph when I laughed and blinked. We laughed until she got hiccups, and then she had to find out, in an experimental mood, if making love would cure hiccups. She said that if it would, it could become a lot more popular than blowing into a paper bag or drinking out of the wrong side of a glass.

On Monday morning as she was scrambling eggs, all dressed for work, she turned to me and said, "Hey!"

"What, honey?"

"I just remembered. It *did* cure those hiccups."

"Yes, but can we patent it?"

She grinned like an urchin. "Maybe not, but we sure know what to do about the next attack."

I patted her and said, "Miss Nina, modern medical science thinks in terms of prevention rather than cure."

She pondered that for a few moments and said, "You know, sweetheart, it's sort of awe-inspiring to think that I may never have another case of hiccups as long as I live. It's the least you can do for me."

She was my joy. She served the eggs and put the pan under the faucet. Then she whirled and with a look of small despair said, "Please tell me, am I too goddam elfin for you?"

"What?"

"Too utterly disgustingly kittenish and prancy and cutey-cute. You know what I mean. Elfin, for God's sake. I just can't be a dignified lady in love—all sighs and swoons. Except for when it's *really* happening, sex with you makes me feel like all games and riots and jokes and prancing. Does it bug you, darling?"

"Not at all."

"I could try to be sort of glamorous."

"Come sit down and eat your eggs before they get cold, you fool woman."

"You do things and it starts me giggling. It's just a sort

77

of a kind of joy, darling. But I don't really want to be a silly child-bride to you."

"Clue me with giggles. Delight me with games. If you were my own device, girl, if I had invented you, geared you, shaped you, wired you for sound, I would have made you exactly what you are in every respect. Does that hold you?"

"Uh huh. But is love supposed to be . . . so much darned fun?"

"Until the prudes came on the scene, it probably always was."

She sat solemnly and ate scrambled eggs for a few minutes, glancing at me, wearing a slight frown.

"Trav?"

"Yes, dear."

"Then maybe what's wrong with me, I worry about enjoying it too much. I like every part of everything. Just even holding you while you sleep makes my heart turn over and over. I want to *be* you. I want us to be one creature, wearing one skin, knowing any pain or pleasure as if we were all of one part. Like once last night, a time when I couldn't reach you, I turned my head like this and kissed my own shoulder, and it made sense to me, and I laughed out loud, because it was our flesh I was kissing with one of our mouths."

I looked at her earnest and troubled face. "Nina, it isn't foolish or wicked to enjoy. Wickedness is hurting people on purpose. I love what you are and how you are and who you are. You give me great joy. And you make horrible coffee."

"I know. Isn't it foul?"

I walked her to work. As we parted she said, "I give you permission to sit on that railing and leer at the Snow Maiden while you wait for me."

"I have a thing about white sweaters."

"Then buy me one. Any fetishes you have, just let me know."

And she joined the throng pouring into the office building.

eight

THAT MONDAY morning, after I had freshened up at my hotel I retrieved Howie's money, took a thousand dollars out of the envelope, taped it up again and had it put back in safekeeping.

Though I felt slightly helpless at penetrating the Currency Curtain the big rich erect around themselves—perhaps to guard them from such as me—I was considerably more confident of my ability to find my way around within the upper level call-girl circuits. Perhaps, though I have never sought such services, this confidence is a clue to the social status of McGee. Once upon a time I had to unravel a situation in Chicago, and I guessed that it could not be too different in New York.

I could assume there would not be too many very fancy and expensive setups. I was not too much concerned about the private entrepreneurs—those little setups where two or three girls are close friends and have enough of the right kind of visiting-fireman contacts to establish themselves on a semi-pro basis. There would be hundreds of those in the city, and they would be too risky for Baynard Mulligan to approve of them. Those girls, not subjected to any outside control, can prove to be neurotic, alcoholic, thieving or diseased. This would have to be a businesslike operation—discreet, reliable, trustworthy, thoroughly screened and paying adequately for all necessary protection. I could not imagine there would be more than three truly expensive circuits in the city.

I hit it on the first try. I tried the Convention Manager of the hotel where I used to stay, before I became so well-known there that I lost some essential freedom of movement. An assistant manager I knew introduced me to the Convention Manager. Even with an introduction he was very edgy and cautious. I told him I had three Venezuelan friends coming to town, and I wanted to line up three very superior girls—

superior, entertaining, fashionable and cooperative—price no object. He hedged and dithered and pretended helplessness, and finally told me I might try Arts and Talents Associates on West 38th Street, and ask for Mrs. Smith, but I was on my own and I could not use his name.

I phoned the place and asked for Mrs. Smith. She had a dull, tired, doughy voice. "Model service, Mrs. Smith speaking."

I said I wanted to employ a model and she asked me if I had an account with them. I said I didn't, but that I wished to open an account. She suggested I stop by and talk with her about it, and if I would be along soon, not to bother stopping at reception but come right to her office, Number 1113.

It was a big drab ugly rabbit-warren of an office building, with noisy elevators, narrow littered corridors. I saw enough of Arts and Talents to see that it was large and busy and very probably entirely legitimate. Kids who looked like theater bums were in groups outside the main entrance to the eleventh-floor offices, drinking Coke and jabbering.

I knocked at 1113 and went in. It was a ten-by-ten office with a single narrow window, a big scarred desk, three phones, a bank of file cabinets, and Mrs. Smith, typing. She was very fat and she had blue hair, stone eyes and a tiny mouth. She did not look evil. She merely looked tired and bored and clerical. She looked at me the way a butcher looks at a side of beef.

"I phoned about opening an account."

"Sit down, please. Excuse me one moment." She finished typing, her fat hands very deft, pulled the sheet out and put it into a manila folder on her desk. She turned and faced me across the desk. "What is your name, please?"

"Maybe you could tell me what the routine is first."

She looked mildly pained. "Our client records are completely confidential. If we open an account for you, you'll be given a code number. There's no cross index to actual names. But I do have to see identification and approve issuing you a code number."

"My name is Travis McGee," I said, and handed her my Florida driver's license.

"Where are you staying in town?" I told her. She asked me to step into the hall until she called me back in. I had about a four-minute wait. She opened the door and nodded and I went back in.

"We don't generally open an account for anyone unless

we have some verification from one of our other accounts. And we also have to know who recommended us."

"The man who recommended you asked me not to use his name. So I'd rather you wouldn't check back with him." She asked who it was. I told her.

"Are you acquainted with any of our other accounts?"

"I believe so. But this is a situation where I would rather not mention names. Would an address be of any help?"

"It might be."

"One twenty-one East Seventy-first. Apartment 9A. I believe it is . . . a current account."

She swiveled around, turning her heavy back toward me. She opened a card drawer. In a few moments she closed it and turned back again. "Yes, of course," she said, and there seemed to be a definite decrease in wariness. "Did that party recommend us also?"

"That party would not be likely to make a specific recommendation, Mrs. Smith. But there were favorable comments about . . . this organization, indirectly."

"We handle small accounts on a cash basis only. And our minimum model fee is two hundred dollars. Will that be satisfactory?"

"Perfectly."

"I believe we can open an account for you. Would you write this number down, please?" I borrowed a pen and wrote it on the margin of one of my permanent credit cards: 90-17. Then she gave me an unlisted number to call, and I wrote that down too.

She rolled a five-by-eight file card into her typewriter and said, "The standard procedure is for you to call that number and give your account number and the time you wish to employ someone, and a number where we can call you back within the hour. I will now fill out your model card, and when you phone in we check this card and then determine availability, make the appointment for you and call you back and give you the details. I'll have to ask you questions about your preferences so that I can complete this card for our records."

"Certainly."

"First, will this be just for normal modeling services? By that I mean you will be the only one involved, and there will be no extremely unusual requirements."

"Just normal by all means."

"Preferable age range?"

"Uh . . . twenty-two to twenty-six."

"Racial type?"

"I beg your pardon?"

"Nordic, Mediterranean, Asiatic, Exotic?"

"Nordic."

"Build?"

"Slim, reasonably tall."

"Any special requirements?"

"Well . . . reasonably bright and presentable."

"All the girls on our list are intelligent, very presentable, smartly dressed, and . . . with the exception of some of the Exotics . . . can be taken anywhere. Many of them have excellent jobs."

"Do you have a space on that card for a sense of humor?"

"You will find that our girls adapt themselves to whatever mood seems required of them. They are lovely girls. Did you say that you wished to employ a model for this evening?"

"If that's possible."

"We do prefer twenty-four hour notice, but there is no particular problem on a Monday night." She turned and rolled her desk chair over to a low filing cabinet. I could see that she was shuffling and sorting photographs, checking them against a list. She turned back to the desk and spread out four eight-by-ten semi-gloss prints for me to examine. I was expecting cheesecake, and was surprised to see that they were head and shoulder shots, studio glamour portraits by someone who knew how to use backlighting. Four very lovely girls, four blonde heads, four sensitive faces. Each portrait had a complicated code number inked in the top right margin.

"These match the information on your model card. If at any time you care to alter your requirements, phone the number I gave you and give your account number and either request a change verbally or come up here and see what we have on file."

"You are certainly beautifully organized here, Mrs. Smith."

"Thank you. We've been in business for a very long time. We can't afford to be slipshod. One of our accounts has been coming in once a year for eleven years to select one of our girls to take on a lengthy cruise—usually thirty to forty days. We handle that on a flat fee of five thousand dollars, so you can readily understand that we must use the greatest care in both the selection of our accounts and the girls on our list. I must tell you that whichever of these girls you select will be asked to make a verbal report on any difficulties. If it is decided that you are not a satisfactory account, your number will be dropped. We owe that much to the girls."

"Of course."

"Which model appeals to you?"

"They're all beautiful. I was wondering, could you tell me if any of these were . . . employed on that other account I mentioned?"

"Why?"

"That's a good question. If one were I thought I'd pick her. Because, as I said, that other client or account—or whatever you call it—was so pleased. Could you check?"

"This is most unusual."

"I don't want to be a nuisance. I'd just feel better about it . . . this first time."

She looked at me with stone eyes and then shrugged. "It will take a few moments to cross-check it." It took longer than a few moments. She sighed heavily from time to time. As she went back to the photo file she said, "Our models also fill out an account-preference card. But I imagine you would be satisfactory to any of them." She turned back to the desk. "Here. None of those original four have been out on that account. These two have, and they match up with your card."

One had a rather ordinarily pretty face and the other looked more interesting. Her face was more angular, slightly vulpine, the upper lids quite plump. "That one," I said.

"You understand, of course, that you must have a place to take her to?"

"I understand."

"Would you wait outside again, please?"

It was a longer wait than before. When she called me in again, she said, "She will meet you this evening at quarter to seven at Satin House on West Forty-eighth. You'll recognize her from her picture. She would prefer it if you get there just a little earlier and sit at the bar so you can see her when she comes in. Her name is Rossa." She spelled it out for me. It was pronounced Raw-sah.

"Last name?"

"Our policy is to leave it up to the girls to give their last name if they so desire. If not, her name is Rossa Smith. She's an enchanting girl. Her model fee is two hundred and fifty dollars. We prefer that you have that amount ready, sealed in a small envelope, and give it to her whenever seems convenient. And I must ask you to leave two hundred dollars with me. It will be posted to your account. It's our protection in case at any time you fail to keep an appointment. Should that happen, we will have to ask you to post another deposit in the same amount before making another appointment. If you don't have the cash, you can bring it to me at any time before five today."

"I have it right here."

"Good. Thank you. If at any time you have any complaint about a model, we would appreciate your bringing it to our attention. I might say that such complaints are very very rare. You will be answered twenty-four hours a day at that number I gave you. Are there any other questions?"

"If I should like Rossa, can I ask for her again?"

"Yes, of course. Many accounts ask for specific girls." She curved her tiny mouth into a small smile. "I'm certain you'll find her most charming. Oh, I forgot to tell you, if at any time you wish to make up a party and require two or more girls, we will appreciate your stopping by and making arrangements in person rather than trying to do it over the phone."

"I understand. Uh . . . how high do the rates go?"

"Most are at two hundred and two-fifty. We have several at three hundred, a few at four hundred, and two at five hundred. But it varies, according to the size and quality of our list at any given time. There have been some at a thousand, but not recently."

"What makes it worth five hundred, Mrs. Smith?"

Her expression told me she thought it a vulgar question. "Those are girls who are very well-known, due to television work usually. Some accounts prefer to be seen with girls who will be recognized in public. Generally they don't stay on our list long." Her smile was quite suddenly and surprisingly vicious. "They either go up, or they go down."

I bade her good day and walked out and found that it was raining, puddling the sidewalks with black city-glop. There were no empty cabs in sight. I went to a corner drugstore. I looked at the pretty girls on the streets, hurrying through the rain. Though I knew it was absurd, they all looked quite different to me. I kept wondering if they were on somebody's list. Behind one fat doughy woman in one small cheap office, I could sense the rest of the organization—the recruiters to bring them in, the suave muscle to keep them in line. It wasn't a sorority. Mrs. Smith wasn't a house mother.

I phoned Terry Drummond from the drugstore. She bellowed hoarse curses at me for almost three minutes before I could quiet her down enough to apologize for not reporting to her about Bonita Hersch.

I made a detailed report. She chided me for being a coward. I said it hadn't been cowardice, merely revulsion.

She said I might have learned something useful. I said that this way there was a better chance of seeing her again. She said she hadn't realized I was so fastidious. She stopped snarling at me when I gave her a hint of what I had in mind and said I would see her in about an hour.

It took a little longer than an hour. A bellhop took over the heavy carton and carried it up to Terry's suite for me. She watched with interest while I unpacked the tape recorder and set it up. It had a two-hour capacity at 3¾ ips, and the operation was very silent. It fit nicely behind the skirts of the sofa, and there was a handy wall plug there for it. I placed it so it was easy to get at the controls from the side of the sofa. I ran the little non-directional microphone up the back of the sofa and pinned it in place just out of sight. I turned it on and we experimented with it, adjusting the gain, talking in different parts of the room, playing the tape back. It would work fine if we could keep the girl in that half of the room. Terry was confident she could get her to sit on the sofa, the ideal place for good pickup.

She had a lot of questions to ask, but not enough time to ask them before a late lunch date. It left me with time to kill. The rain had stopped. I had a sandwich and then I went down to take a look at the Armister layout. It was on a narrow side street in the financial district, a sooty old gray two-story building with ornate stone work around the cornices. There were three stone steps up to a dignified entrance doorway. A brass plate set into the stone at the side of the entrance said "Armister-Hawes" in fragile and ancient script worn thin by many polishings. There was a uniformed porter to keep things swept and polished, and to open the door for the people.

I found a pay phone in an office building a block away and called Nina and told her I might be fairly late, and to get herself fed and be patient.

"I'd hate to start before you get there," she said.

"It's a very old joke and I'm surprised you know it."

"I plan to be a constant source of surprises and consternations, McGee."

"Your record so far is excellent. How about your busted door. Did you phone the man?"

"It's being fixed today. What's so interesting you can't be home when I get there?"

"I've lined up a tall blonde."

"I don't think I'm keeping you busy enough, dear."

"Go on back to the old drawing board."

"I got my bonus. It's a pretty blue check. And I got pinched in the elevator again. Does that mean anything?"

"I'll tell you what it means when I see you late tonight."

As I hung up I had a tantalizing memory which for a moment I could not identify. Then I remembered the rude, random conversations I'd had on field telephones long ago with Mike Gibson. That memory was like taking an unexpected blow right over the heart. I wondered why Nina and I had not talked more about Mike. Maybe she sensed that it would make me feel strange and guilty. She did not want to be the picture of the twelve-year-old girl in Mike's wallet. I did not see how she could be. They could not be one and the same. No.

But I fed coins into the box and sent Mike a wire, for the nurse to read to him. EVERYTHING SHAPING UP BETTER THAN YOU THOUGHT. DETAILS SOON. I felt like a sneak when I sent it. "Shake her up if you have to, Trav," Mike had said. Thanks a lot, buddy.

I roamed back past Armister-Hawes, on the opposite side of the street, wondering if I could chance going in and saying hello to Bonita, wondering what good it would do. After I passed it, I glanced back just in time to see a big black Lincoln pull up in front. A huge, husky chauffeur in a blue-gray uniform got out slowly. I moved into a handy doorway and watched the scene. It was twenty minutes of four. He wandered around the car, stopped and took a handkerchief out and rubbed a place on the window trim. The porter came out and they stood and talked idly. The porter kept glancing back through the glass doors. Suddenly he turned and hurried up the steps and pulled the door open, half-bowing, smiling, touching his cap. Two men and a woman came out. The woman was Bonita Hersch, in a dark tailored office suit, with a puff of white at her throat. Both men looked tanned and fit, tailored and prosperous. One was tall and lean, with a long face and a long neck and sloping shoulders. He wore no hat. He had white hair, curled tightly and closely to his skull. The other man was shorter and broader. He wore a dark hat and a pale topcoat. The chauffeur was holding the rear door of the car open. The taller man walked slowly toward the car. The broader man stopped and said something to the porter. The porter responded. The man threw his head back and laughed. He punched the porter on the shoulder, and then did a little dance step, fists up, in a parody of boxing. Bonita tugged at his arm. The man turned and went with her toward the car, laughing again. They got in and the chauffeur closed the door and hurried around the back of the car and got behind the wheel. The big gleaming car started up smoothly and moved away down the wet street.

I hurried over. The porter was just going back inside. He saw me and held the door for me. He was much older than he had looked from a distance.

"Wasn't that Miss Hersch who just drove off?"

"Yes sir, her and Mr. Mulligan and young Mr. Armister. They're gone for the day now, sir."

"*Young* Mr. Armister?"

He looked embarrassed. "It's just a habit. He's the only Mr. Armister nowadays."

"Would Miss Morse still be here?"

"Oh yes sir, she won't be leaving till five or after. You go right straight down this main hall, sir, and turn left at the end and her desk is there right out in the open outside Miss Hersch's office."

I thanked him and went back. Angela Morse was an overweight little sandy blonde with a nervous expression and a bad complexion. As she looked at me apprehensively, I told her that I knew I had just missed Miss Hersch, and I would like to leave a personal note for her, if she could give me something to write on. She gave me pad and pen with fumbling haste.

I wrote, "Stopped by to buy you a coffee break only to find out you keep very executive hours. I'm wishing myself better luck next time. Trav."

She gave me an envelope for it, and I put the note in and gave it back, unsealed. She said she would put it on Miss Hersch's desk. She wore a navy-blue something with a white schoolgirl collar. The offices had a hushed and sepulchral flavor of money. The ceilings were high, the carpeting deep, the paneling dark and glossy and carved. Through an open door I could see into the rigid formality of a small conference room. Angela Morse's desk was set up in sort of an inner foyer, a wide formal central area onto which the other executive offices opened. There was a crystal chandelier, a small fireplace. A small display light shone on an oil painting in a ornate gilt frame. I suddenly realized that it certainly was not a reproduction of Manet haystacks. Perhaps a copy? I moved over and read the little plaque on the frame. Manet. The girl's electric typewriter stopped. It was a brash snickety little sound in that setting. I turned and she was looking at me, apparently wondering why I didn't leave.

"This is a handsome room," I said.

"It's kind of spooky, not getting hardly any daylight in here to work by."

"Do they use both floors?"

"No. I mean sort of. It's storage up there for supplies and all, and dead old files that go back a thousand years practically. And a dusty old apartment nobody has used in years."

"I thought it was a lot bigger organization."

"Counting everybody, there's twenty-three now. It used to be about thirty-five last year. But we don't manage as many properties now."

"I imagine Mr. Armister is a nice guy to work for."

She smiled. "Oh, he's real nice. He's kind of jolly and fun and all. He isn't at all stuffy like you'd think."

Jolly Charlie Armister. Just a rich bundle of fun. Fun with Bonita. Fun with the Arts and Talents.

I thanked her again and walked slowly down the center corridor, glancing into the offices on either side, at the mild sedate girls running the chuckling electric machinery that recorded the flux of money, at the quiet men making little marks on tabulated reports and talking in bank voices into phones and dictation equipment. It was the world's most dignified horse-room. The basic commodity was the same.

After those offices, my hotel looked like something designed to be thrown away after use. The old city was being filled with these tall tasteless rectangles, bright boxes which diminished the people who had to live and work in them. People kennels. Disposable cubicles for dispensable people. As I showered I wondered if perhaps these hideous new tax-shelter buildings, with people sealed into the sour roar of manufactured air, didn't play some significant part in creating New York's ever-increasing flavor of surly and savage bitterness—a mocking wise-guy stink of discontent. Ugliness creates more ugliness. So the buildings could contribute, and so could the narrow greed of the truly vicious little trade unions. Screw you, buster, I'm getting mine. Thirty-hour week. Twenty-five-hour week. Grind the last panicky dime out of the golden goose. So it's down to twenty-five hours, which figures to ten bucks an hour, and anybody gets smart—all you do is walk out again and tie up the whole crappy city. But even when you're working, what do you do with all those great raw boring horrible hunks of time? All those hours when if anybody looks at you just a little bit wrong, you want to smash them to pulp. Man, we got a strong union. We got this city right by the balls. But something is going wrong and nobody knows exactly what it is. You can read it in all the eyes you see.

nine

THE SATIN HOUSE was jammed with glossy people in that kind of lighting which makes women look mysterious and men look stalwart. Smiles and glassware sparkled. Some huge suction yanked the smoke up and out. Soft accoustics blurred and merged all the shoulder-to-shoulder yakking. I got a stool at the very end of the bar near the door, my right shoulder against the wall, and a huge tailored back at my left blocking all vision in that direction. The bartenders made their deft moves between the gleaming bottle rack and the dark wood and red leather of the bar.

I kept a full drink in front of me, and I kept craning my head around to watch the door. She came in precisely on time, looking for no one, knowing in perfect confidence she would be looked for; tall, but not quite as tall as I had guessed from her face; slender in a dark green-gray wool dress; a mutation mink jacket that matched almost perfectly the taffy pallor of her hair; a hat that would have been hilarious worn by anyone without that look of remote and lovely calm; big lizard purse with silver clasp, lizard shoes.

I went to her quickly. "Rossa, you're right on time."

"Hello!" she said with smile, with a warmth as subtle as her perfume.

"I'm Trav, and there's one tiny corner over there I've been hoarding."

I took her over. Broad-back had taken my stool. He was turned, facing his companion. "Excuse me," I said. He gave me a totally disinterested glance and went on talking to his friend.

"Excuse me," I said again. This time he did not even glance.

I was getting very tired of this city. I had heard his friend call him Bernie. I put my fingertips on his chin and turned his face around toward me. He clapped his hand on my wrist to pull my arm down. I was braced and he could have chinned himself on it without depressing it a quarter-inch.

"Bernie," I said, "lift it off my stool or I am going to make a rude and terrible scene. I might bite one of your pretty ears right off." The bartender had moved close and I could sense the management behind me.

"Oh, were you sitting here?" he said. It was his most plausible decision. He got up. He went around and stood on the other side of his friend. He laughed very very heartily. He showed his shiny teeth when he laughed. Rossa slid onto my stool and asked for a sweet vermouth on the rocks. I wedged in beside the stool, arm on the bar, facing toward her.

"I don't really go around stirring up trouble," I said.

"I would have run," she said. "I am a sissy." She had a very slight accent, possibly Danish or Scandinavian. When she had walked, when she had slid onto the stool, she had moved well, in a flowing and limber manner. Her face was angular and distinctive, with the planes and hollows of handsomeness rather than the round look of prettiness. Her brows were darker than her hair, arched highly in an habitual expression of mild query. Her upper lids were so full as to narrow and tilt her eyes, gray and as pale as mine. The skin texture of her face was very fine, and she used a slightly orange shade of lipstick on the full broad mouth.

"It's stuffy in here, Rossa. Should I check your jacket?"

"Do you want to stay very long in a place so crowded, Trav?" She tasted my name as she said it, with a slight hesitation.

"I guess not."

"Then I am fine, thank you. There's a place near for a drink, not so crowded, where we can both sit. Unless you have some other place you would rather go?"

"We'll try your place."

She wrinkled her nose in a small smile. "We will drink quickly and let Bernie have the stool, eh? Then he will be a big man again."

We walked a half block to another place. She had a nice long stride. There was a small blue booth for two along a dark wall. She chatted easily. She told me her name was Rossa Hendit, and she worked in an airlines ticket office on Fifth Avenue. She did not say which one. I could imagine some such name as Swenska or Nordway or Fiordlund, one of those little tiled places with a shiny engine in the window and pieces of ribbon leading to strange names on a map.

I told her I was from Florida. She had been to Miami several times. We talked climate, citrus, beaches and sunburn lotion. She had no whore look or whore manner that I could detect. But there was a curious inadequacy about our easy conversation. We both knew there was an envelope of money in one of my pockets, and it would end up in her purse. This was a situation I had never been in before. It took me a long time to analyze it. Finally I realized that we could generate no particular tension between us because the result was preordained. She was a stately and beautiful girl, fashionable and bright, with shining eyes and a good mouth. But there was no spice of pursuit. A doe which runs up and stares down the gun barrel is not a sporting venture. There is an electric tension in the chase, in searching out the little clues and vulnerabilities, making those little adjustments which favor the hunter. The biggest question had been answered before we met. Mrs. Smith had been the one who said yes. The only remaining question was how she would be in bed. And from the look of her, and from the cost of her, I could be certain she would be smooth-skinned, sensuous, tasty, and just as active or as passive as anybody wanted her to be. She looked as if she had passionate capacity, but one would never know whether her responses would be genuine or faked. I guessed she had begun judging and appraising me from the first moment and was, and would continue to be, trying to react in all ways which would please me. She wished, or had been taught, to give full value.

At one point I glanced up quickly and surprised a different expression in her eyes—an absolute coldness, a bleak and total indifference which was gone the instant I saw it. And that, I thought, was the whore's look and the whore's secret, that monumental unconcern which insulated her. I knew in that moment that this sort of thing could never interest me. I had to have the involvement of the spirit. These tasty goods were for other kinds of men: the ones for whom sex is an uncomplicated physical function one performs with varying degrees of skill with every broad and chick who will hold still for it; the men who are the cigar chompers, gin players, haunch-grabbers; the loud balding jokesters with several deals going for them on the long-distance lines; the broad-bellied expense-account braggards who grab the checks, goose the cocktail waitresses, talk smut, and run-run-run until their kidneys quit or their hearts explode.

And this savory and expensive chick had decorated the night places with them, and had lost track of the number of bald heads, lost track of the number of times she had, with the cigar smouldering on the night stand, skilfully drained their transient loins.

Into a small silence I said, "Have you been doing this long?"

The answer came so quickly and reasonably it had the ring of policy. "Dear, don't think of such things. You'll make us both unhappy. I work all day. I like to go out. I'm your date."

"It's just a little friendly curiosity, Rossa."

"Please, dear, with you I have been feeling that it is really a date. Let me keep pretending."

"You mean we're different, you and I?"

"Don't you feel that way about it too, darling?"

It was very skilled. As standard practice it would inflate the man's ego. Every man could be led to believe he was special. And at the end, with a great faked galloping climax, she would make him believe it forever. Every customer is unique.

"Perhaps. But I want to talk about it."

She pouted in a rather pretty way, and said, "How did a lovely girl like you get into anything like this? Isn't that a very trite question, Trav? Aren't you and I worth better conversation than that?"

"Do you know that old joke, what the lovely girl answers?"

"Surely. Just lucky, I guess. Darling, it is really very adolescent of you to want to pry. Just accept me. As if I was born an hour ago, just for you."

"All clean and fresh and sweet and virginal."

She looked down at her hand. She examined the nails. It reminded me of Bonita Hersch's hand, except that the nails were longer. She looked across at me. This time the whore look was frank and apparent. Under all that tasty trimming was a basic coarseness which would gag a goat. I didn't have to know how she got into the business. It had been invented for her.

"If you can wait here an hour, someone will come who might suit you better. One of the newer ones, I think. Younger and possibly a little nervous about everything."

"I wasn't trying to offend you, Rossa."

"My dear fellow, it would stagger the imagination to think of any way you could possibly offend me. I was merely thinking of making things more agreeable for you."

"You are agreeable."

Suddenly her smile was dazzling. She was a fashion model facing into an imaginary spring breeze in a professional studio. "I will suit you very very well. Never fear. You are an exciting man, Trav. I shouldn't want to give you up at this point. Now we can forget all that and this will be a date for us. You came in to buy a ticket. You asked me to have a drink with you after work. I am a very proper girl and I am wondering if you are going to make me feel too reckless." She reached with a small gold lighter and lit my cigarette and then, as she started to hold the flame to her own, fumbled with it and it dropped into her lap and clattered onto the floor. She laughed and said, "See? You are actually making me a little bit nervous, darling."

I sat on my heels beside our small blue booth and peered under the table for the lighter. I saw the glint of it back against the wall and reached and picked it up, sat back in the booth, lit her cigarette with it and handed it to her.

"Thank you, dear," she said, with a splendid imitation of fondness.

We finished our drinks, ordered another.

I felt incomparably shrewd. I would take her to the Plaza. I would take her up to Terry's suite and suddenly Rossa Hendit would discover that it was not the sort of evening she had anticipated. All we wanted from her was conversation about Charlie, and Terry was set up to pay well for it. The tape would furnish Terry's very good lawyer with enough background to enable him to go after a court order to get Charles McKewn Armister hospitalized for observation, with Joanna Armister signing the commitment papers. After they had taken him off whatever they had him on, Charlie would be able to blow the whole scheme sky high.

My date began to seem slightly absent-minded. It was a quiet bar, and thinning out. She went to the ladies' room and seemed to be gone a long time.

Reality is a curious convention. It is the special norm for each of us. Based upon the evidences of our own senses, we have each established our own version of reality. We are constantly rechecking it with all sensory equipment. In the summer of 1958 I was in Acapulco when a major earthquake struck that area. I was awakened by the grating of roof tiles and a thousand dogs howling. I went barefoot to the window. There was a cool tile floor under my bare feet. Suddenly I realized that the tile floor was rippling. There were waves in the solid tile, throwing me off balance. Such a thing could not be. Tile floors were solid. To have such a floor rippling in such a way destroyed the validity of all sensory impressions, and gave me a feeling of black and

94

primitive terror I had never felt before. I could no longer depend upon my evidences of reality.

She came back from the ladies' room. She sat and smiled at me. I said, "Let's get another drink up at the Plaza."

That is what my mind told my mouth to say. But the fit of the words in my mouth felt strange. I heard, like an after-echo, what I had said. "Let's get a down with the ending ever."

She was leaning toward me, with a narrow and curious avidity. "Darling," she said. "Darling, darling." It had an echo-chamber quality. She opened her mouth wide enough so that I could see the pink curl of her tongue as she formed the *d*.

I saw a tiny mark appear at her hair line, right in the center of her forehead. It moved slowly down her forehead, and as it did so the two flaps of flesh folded away at either side, bloody pink where they were exposed, displaying the hard white shine of ivory bone. The moving line parted her brows, bisected her nose and lips and chin, and the halved damp soft flesh fell away leaving the white skull, the black sockets where the eyes had been. The jaws and teeth were exposed in a white death grin, but the jaw still worked and the pink tongue was still moist within that sepulchral dryness, curling, saying, "Darling, darling."

I closed my eyes tightly, both hands clamped on the edge of the table. Under my hands the table edge turned wet and soft and full of roundnesses. I squinted down, fighting for control, and with vision it turned back into a table edge. But as I closed my eyes again all the softness was under my hands. This was the earthquake terror again, roaring through my mind like a black wind. In some far corner of my mind I was trying to make an appraisal. She had dropped the lighter and kicked it over against the wall. It gave her time enough.

I tried to hang onto a tiny edge of reality. I knew the words. I wanted the whole room to hear the words. Call the police.

I heard the words come out. A wet, brutish howling. "Can Paul bury shit anything." My muscles were knotted. I risked a glance at the skull. She was gone. She seemed gone. I could not be sure she was gone. I could not be sure of anything.

Then the room tilted abruptly, thudding my shoulder against the wall. I tried to see them. They were in a half-circle standing on that steep slant, looking down into the booth, the tallest narrowest people I had ever seen, with tiny little heads no bigger than oranges. One of them was a policeman. "Hadda!" I yelled at him. "Hassa hadda," and began to vomit

95

with fright. A snake looked at me out of a door in the cop's narrow belly.

Then there were white things, white grunting things, running at me and pulling, and I fought them in a dream, and was yanked and mashed face down and felt a little stinging bite in my buttock.

I rolled under a night sky and saw a thousand tiny peering faces at either side, atop tall inleaning bodies. There was a thump, a sliding, a bang of doors. Motor roar. High city lights moving by. A sinking deepness, somebody close by and fingers on my wrist. The thing I was in turned on its side and we went off into dark country, scraping swiftly along on the side, leaving a shower of sparks . . .

For a long time I could not tell whether I was awake or asleep. I was in a bed in a white room. Daylight came through a window screened with heavy mesh. I could move my head, and that was all. I could see a white wall. Things kept happening to that wall. For a long time I could not stop them from happening. In sleep you cannot stop things from happening. Places would open in the wall. I could see into horrid places and see horrid things. Grotesque copulations. Huge rotting bugs. Ghastly things eating each other. Things would open the wall from the other side and come through and disappear as they got too close to the bed, and I would go rigid waiting for them to get me. Once hundreds of people started laughing at me. They were behind the bed where I could not see them. It was deafening.

After an interval of time I could not measure, I began to be able to exert control over the wall. I could close it up and make it white and blank. It was like making a fist with my mind. If I let the fist relax, the things would come again. After a long time I began to be able to relax the fist little by little without anything appearing. I became convinced that I was awake. Later I was able to make ghastly things appear only by an effort of will, a kind of reaching to make them happen. They lost color and solidity. Finally I could make nothing happen. I was in a white room. I was in bed. I could move only my head.

Two men came in. They stood by the bed and looked down at me. One was in a business suit. He had a bald head and a young face. The other was tall, young and husky, dressed in white.

The one in the business suit said, "How do you feel?"

"Who are you?"

"I am Doctor Varn. I'd like to know if you are still hallucinating."

My mind seemed to take a long time to grasp the question and find the answer. "No. There aren't any things in the wall any more."

"Do you hear any strange sounds?"

"Not any more. Where am I?"

"Toll Valley Hospital, Mr. McGee, just south of New Paltz, New York. It is a private institution for the treatment of mental and nervous disorders."

"Why am I here?"

"Because you are ill, Mr. McGee. Jerry, please go tell Dr. Moore we can schedule Mr. McGee for hypno-therapy at two o'clock."

The one in white left. I heard the door close.

"I'm not sick."

"You were very ill, Mr. McGee. You were irrational and violent in front of witnesses, including an officer of the law. In New York State any officer of the law can commit you for observation if he is a witness to dangerous and irrational behavior, if, in his opinion you are endangering public safety."

I wished my brain did not feel so slow and tired and muddy. "Then . . . wouldn't I go to a public hospital?"

"Usually, yes. But I have been treating you for some time now, Mr. McGee. When you began to behave oddly, your friend, Miss Hendit, became alarmed and phoned me. I arranged to have you brought out here."

"You have been treating me for some time?"

"According to my office files. My nurse can verify it, of course." He shook his head. "Until last evening, I really thought we were making progress."

He was so plausible it frightened me as badly as the things in the wall. I forced myself back toward reality. "What did that whore put into my drink?"

"That's an irrational question, Mr. McGee."

"So give me an irrational answer. Humor me."

"In the past several years we've made some very interesting discoveries regarding the relationship between blood chemistry and mental disorders. In order to get the extreme reaction you experienced, she would have had to give you quite a dangerous dosage of a complex chemical compound which can, in a normal human being, temporarily duplicate all the physical and mental and sensory symptoms of violent schizophrenia."

"But she didn't have to do that because I was already nuts."

He looked down at me with mild surprise and a certain amount of approval. "Mr. McGee, you have astonishing recuperative powers—mental and physical. You broke the arm of a very highly-trained attendant."

"Good."

"I expected you to be slightly incoherent, but your word choice seems controlled. We can schedule you sooner than I expected."

"For that therapy you told him about?"

"Dr. Moore uses a combination of mild hypnotic drugs and hypnotic technique. You see, we need to know a great deal more about you, Mr. McGee. We are particularly interested in all of your activities during the past several days."

"I won't tell you a damned thing."

"That is an irrational statement. But perhaps I made an inaccurate statement. We are not particularly interested in your activities. We have a request for an accurate report of your activities. We are far more interested in your responses to the psychotomimetic drugs."

"The what?"

"Our resident organic chemist, Doctor Daska, had been achieving some interesting variations in the Hofmann formulae, creating more directive compounds in the psilocybin and D-lysergic acid diethylamide areas. The experimental compound the girl gave you has the lab designation of Daska-15. A single odorless tasteless drop. Approximately three-millionths of an ounce, actually, in a distilled-water suspension. Harvard University's Center for Research in Personality has done some basic work in this area, but Daska can achieve more predictability. Daska-15 gives consistently ugly hallucinations, and mimics highly psychotic disturbances of the sensory areas, communication and so on." He seemed to have forgotten he was talking to me. His enthusiasm and dedication were apparent.

"What the hell kind of a place *is* this?" I demanded.

His young face firmed as he brought his attention back from the misty distances of research.

"Eh? Oh, this is the Mental Research Wing of Toll Valley Hospital, Mr. McGee. We're concerned with psychotomimetic techniques, surgical techniques, electrical and chemical stimulation of areas of the brain—in fact the whole range of the mechanical rather than the psychiatric approach to mental disorder."

"What the hell kind of a doctor are you? You know I don't belong here."

"We're making significant progress in several directions. Important progress." He seemed strangely apologetic, and anxious for me to understand.

"So what?"

"We have chimps and monkeys and rodents who didn't ask to come here either, Mr. McGee."

My mind was quickening a little. "Are you trying to tell me I'm some kind of an experimental animal?"

"All this work is generously supported by foundation money."

Were I a character in a funnypaper, a light bulb would have appeared over my head. "One of the Armister foundations?"

He looked sad and apologetic. "Crash programs are essential in this area, Mr. McGee. It is . . . a very difficult thing to weigh a few isolated instances of . . . questionable ethical behavior against the greatest good for the greatest number. Also . . ." His voice trailed off into a trouble silence.

"Also what?"

"It would be illegal to attempt to solicit healthy volunteers. And the few cases we can get from the main hospital, with all necessary permissions, are generally so hopeless we can't accurately appraise results." He shrugged a mild sadness away and smiled down at me, his features clean and remarkably handsome under the sheen of his hairless head. "We're not monsters, Mr. McGee. There won't be anything as unpleasant as what you have already been through. Many of the Daska compounds have extremely pleasant side effects. This will merely be a case of taking you through the experimental series, and then, under hypnotics, getting your detailed verbal report of the experience and sensations. You'll be physically checked and checked against the electro-encephalograph and given a detailed multiphasic personality inventory test between each segment of the series to determine any area of deterioration."

"You are so comforting, Doctor. Was Charles Armister here?"

He hesitated and said, "He was with us for ten weeks." He looked at his watch. "I'll send in some medication, and some people to get you cleaned up and fed, Mr. McGee."

"You want to keep me healthy."

"Yes, of course," he said, and smiled and nodded and went out.

I had ten minutes alone. McGee, the suave shrewd operator. In retrospect I could marvel at the heights of blundering stupidity I had reached. It was as if a team of experts were systematically looting a bank, and I had come bumbling onto the scene to ask them how they were making out.

Certainly Mrs. Smith of Arts and Talents had checked with the other account. It gave them the time, place and opportunity to get me out of their hair. Probably before that they had become aware of my buzzing around, drinking with Bonita, leaving her a note at the office, getting in contact with Terry Drummond, talking to the law about Howard Plummer, getting close to Plummer's fiancee. So when my buzzing became a little too annoying, they had swatted me. And I hadn't even taken the very elementary precaution of leaving some record of what I had learned, where it could get into the hands of the law.

Suddenly I felt a fear quite different from the terror of any distortion of reality. I was afraid for Nina Gibson and what they could do to her if she tried to do anything about my inexplicable disappearance.

A square sandy woman in white came in, bared my shoulder, held a hypo up to the light, then injected me in the shoulder muscle. She did not speak when spoken to. She swabbed the spot with alcohol before and after the injection and went away. In a little while I chuckled. I felt very very good. What the hell, let them have their fun. It was for the good of mankind. Way down in my mind a little lizard-head of fright kept opening its cupboard and looking out, but I kept shoving it back. I locked the cupboard door. Two husky attendants came in. They got me up, took me out of the canvas jacket. I wanted to apologize for mussing my bed. I didn't want to be a burden to anybody. They were arguing with each other about the season bets they were going to make on pro football. I wanted to tell them a joke to make them laugh with me, but I couldn't think of one. They took me into a adjoining tiled bath. I stripped on request and they put me into a shower and gave me soap and a brush. I hummed as I showered. When I came out they gave me a coverall suit to wear, a light-green garment zippered from throat to crotch. It seemed the most wonderfully practical and comfortable thing I had ever worn. I couldn't understand why everyone didn't wear exactly the same thing. They gave me straw slippers. Instead of telling me what to do, they tended to give me a shove in the direction they wanted me to go. I didn't mind. They were busy talking to each other. One of them thought the Packers could do it again.

I sat on the bed. They put the wheeled tray in front of me. I had to eat everything with a hard rubber spoon. Everything was delicious. They stood by the screened window and talked. Whenever one would glance toward me, I would smile. But they didn't seem to notice the smile or want to be friends. That was all right too. When I was finished, one of them took me back into the bathroom and produced an electric razor. He watched me until he was certain I could use it properly. I was anxious to use it properly, to please him.

They took me down a hall. It was a gray hall, like ships I had been on. I had a quick look out one window and saw a nice place of lawns and trees, flowers and a parking lot far away, and some people strolling on the paths. It was a very nice place.

They took me to a room. Dr. Varn was there. I was glad to see him again. His friend was named Dr. Moore. He was a nice fellow too, a middle-sized man like Doctor Varn, but swarthy. They had me get into a lounging chair and then they fixed it so that I was very very comfortable. They darkened the room. Dr. Moore started a tiny light swinging in a circle above me. I watched the light. Dr. Moore told me I was very comfortable. He had a nice voice. Friendly. He was interested in me. I was very anxious to please him. In all that comfort I closed my eyes and folded back into myself, as if looking down into the blackness inside my head. I could hear my voice and his voice, and they were a little bit apart from me. I could tell Dr. Moore everything. It is good to have someone you can tell everything to. It is good to have someone who is concerned about you. I told him all my troubles, but they did not really seem very important any more. If anything was wrong, he would fix it.

ten

IT WAS night again. Lights came on in my room. Dr. Varn shook me, and I came awake suddenly. I rolled out of bed and came to my feet. Varn backed away. He had two attendants with him. A different pair. They looked wary and competent.

"Oh, you bastards," I said. "You sick dirty bastards."

"Mr. McGee, you can be reasonable or you can be unreasonable. If you are unreasonable, we'll put you under restraint. There is someone here to talk to you. There is something he wants you to do. And you have to be alert and awake to do what he wants. He is certain you will want to do it."

I slowly brought myself under control. I had nothing to gain by getting my hands on Varn.

"I'll be reasonable," I said. It was an effort.

"Come with me, please."

The attendants came too. There were small lights in the corridors, like battle lamps. We went down narrow concrete stairs. I was trying to learn as much as I could about the layout.

We went to a small visiting room. They herded me into a metal chair. It was bolted to the floor. They pulled a wide strap like a seat belt across my thighs, and made it fast. When they started to fasten my arms to the arms of the chair, Varn told them not to bother. He sent one away. He told one to watch me. He went out and came back in a few moments with the same man I had seen getting into the Lincoln with Armister and Bonita Hersch.

He had a long face and a long neck. At first glance he looked frail. But sloping shoulders packed the fabric of the tailored suit, and his hands were big and knuckly, his wrists heavy. His white hair was curly, fitting the long skull closely—

a dramatic cap of silver. He had a look of cool intelligence. Of importance.

He stood, and without taking his eyes off me, said, "Doctor, if you and your man would wait outside the door, please. I'll sing out if we have any difficulty in here. I don't think we will."

Varn and the attendant went out. The man said, "You do know who I am, of course."

"Baynard Mulligan."

He hitched himself onto a steel table and sat facing me, long legs swinging. "I will have to take Varn's word that you are highly intelligent. You've made belief a little difficult, McGee."

"I'm not used to such rarified atmosphere, Mr. Mulligan."

"You could have figured certain things out for yourself, certain obvious equations. This venture is about ten times as profitable as anything you have ever heard of before. So it was planned for ten times as long, is conducted with ten times the care, and has ten times as many safeguards against interference. Fortunately there are not ten times as many people involved. That would increase the risk and diminish the return."

"How many are involved?"

"Nine of us, to a greater or lesser degree. Say five principals and four assistants. It's very complex."

"How are you making out?"

"We're on schedule. Not too much greed and not too little. A proper amalgam of boldness and caution. In addition to all operating expenses, we've diverted six millions of dollars to established number accounts in Zurich. We're under continuous tax audit of course, which you might call the official seal of approval. Another eighteen months should see us home free—target twenty millions. That is just about the maximum amount we can cover with the faked portfolios and fictitious holdings. Not the maximum, actually. I always insist upon a safety factor. Our Mr. Penerra advises me that it will take years to discover through audit all the ways we managed it and covered our tracks. By then, of course, all five principals will be happily and comfortably distributed in extradition-proof areas. You see, when an applecart gets so big, McGee, one man is a fool to expect to tip it over. What's the matter? You look upset."

"You're telling me a lot."

"Yes, I guess you are reasonably bright. I wouldn't be telling you this if there was the slightest possible chance of your telling anyone else. I assure you, there is not the slightest possible chance. So, if you care to ask questions?"

"If this is such a careful, cautious, brilliant operation, how come you handled Plummer so stupidly? That's what brought me into it."

"I know. Bitter, heartbroken girl, and your duty to poor Mike and so on. Quite touching, actually. But you see, Mc-Gee, it was just a curious kind of irony. There was a slight lack of judgment involved. Plummer had a good head. He was becoming troublesome. I tried to talk him into resigning. Simplifying of our operations, no future and so forth. Finally he agreed. I had offered him a five-thousand-dollar bonus at termination. He asked for ten. It seemed strange. He wanted it in cash. That was easily arranged. I thought I knew what he had in mind. Childish, really, but it could have worked. He planned to go to the tax people with it, claim something funny was going on but that he had no proof, and drop the cash on a desk and ask them why he could ask for and get a cash bonus in that amount if his suspicions were incorrect. We had him followed. We found out that he had arranged an appointment. We could not let him keep it, of course. We were set up to have him brought here, under very plausible circumstances. But before it could be finalized that same evening, the poor fellow was actually mugged. By person or persons unknown."

"You didn't have him killed?"

"Don't be a fool. It was an ironic accident. We're too bright and too civilized to be murderous, McGee. This is a business operation. If you have been thinking you would be killed, allow me to ease your mind."

"Do you expect to keep me here forever?"

"That would be too awkward and too expensive. McGee, we are actually in your debt. Things were going so smoothly that we became slightly careless. It was good for us to have you arrive on the scene. Through your efforts we have learned that Olan Harris—the chauffeur, and one of our assistants in this project—has been dangerously stupid. Searching those apartments is unforgivable. For ten thousand dollars he endangered a project concerned with two thousand times that amount. He said he just kept thinking about that money. He is already in residence in this wing. Varn is delighted to get him. He is as hardy a physical specimen as you are, McGee. Poor Varn keeps deploring the fact he can't publish his test findings."

"And is Miss Hersch here too?"

104

"You are quick, aren't you? She is not subject to that sort of disposal. Or, to be a little more accurate, perhaps, not subject to disposal until the operation is terminated. She is essential. Mr. Armister is dependent upon her. She handles him nicely. Miss Hersch is not exactly a principal, though she believes herself to be. Her behavior in this matter had been very regrettable. She is a snob, of course. She went running when Mrs. Drummond summoned her. She took you at face value. She got drunk. She told you too much, far too much. She admitted all this, admitted she had been foolish, and promised it would never happen again. She did not admit her attempt to arrange to have intercourse with you. But it became quite obvious from what you told Dr. Moore. She is contrite. But I think we can arrange a very suitable discipline for her. Very suitable. It should quiet any random urges she might have been feeling."

"What's going to happen to me?"

"Nothing, until we can be certain no one is going to make a fuss about you, McGee. Varn and Moore and Daska will run tests on you. You shouldn't suffer any damage from those. And when the time seems appropriate, you will be treated and released."

The very casualness of his tone made me feel chilled.

"That word 'treated' intrigues me."

"It has made Mr. Armister a very contented man, McGee."

"What has?"

"It's a minor surgery. It used to be used frequently in cases of acute anxiety, but it has been discredited these past few years. I can only give you my layman's idea of it, of course. Varn used to do a lot of them. They go in at the temples, I believe, with a long thin scalpel and stir up the frontal lobes. It breaks the old behavior patterns in the brain. With a normal adult it has very specific effects. It will drop your intelligence quotient about forty points, permanently. It will make you incontinent at first. They'll shift you over to one of the regular rooms for special care—toilet training, dressing and feeding yourself, that sort of thing. You will have a short attention span, but you will be able to make a living doing some kind of routine task under supervision. It does cure all repressions and inhibitions, McGee. You will become a very friendly earthy fellow. Very strong but quite casual sex impulses. You will eat well and sleep well, and you will have no tendency to fret or worry about anything. If somebody annoys you, you may react a little too violently, but other than that you should have no trouble with society. It will be a pleasant life, believe me. Mr. Armister is quite content. We keep him well-dressed and tanned and healthy, and see that he has a chance to satisfy all random desires. In return he signs his name wherever he is asked to. And he creates a nice impression. He isn't very rewarding to talk to for any great length of time, but he passes muster when he sits in on signings and conferences. Most important of all, McGee, you will have just small disorganized memories of all this, and no urge to do anything about anything you do happen to remember clearly. Mr. Armister remembers his wife and children, but has no urge to see them."

I could not speak. There were no words to convey my horror at what they had done to him. And wanted to do to me.

"Charlie is a powerful man," he said quietly. "He led a life of sexual repression and torment. Now he is extremely active, but without what Miss Hersch terms finesse. In the beginning we thought she could provide everything he would need. But after a month she begged off, and we agreed to supply Charlie with girls he could use. It's a minor expense compared with the return which comes from keeping him content. But now, I think, that as a sort of continuous act of contrition, Miss Hersch will assume her prior duties and functions. At any rate, there is something I wish you to do. We have checked you out of the hotel. I want you to write two letters. Varn will bring the necessary materials. You will write to Florida and arrange to have your boat sold and the money and your personal possessions shipped here."

"You're crazy as hell."

"And you will write to Miss Nina Gibson and tell her that you are not interested in pursuing this further, and wish her well, and quiet her suspicions. A nice pleasant and rather chilly brush-off. Actually, a note to Mike Gibson might be in order too. And one to Terry Drummond? I don't know. I'll have to think about that. She is just a little too important and well-known to tangle with. Personally, I think she'll get bored and say the hell with it and go back to Greece."

"I will not write a damned word to anybody."

"Varn!"

The door burst open so quickly I knew my chances of trying anything were slim. And I had the feeling that in the last twenty-four hours I had lost a small edge of physical coordination. When Varn and the attendant saw nothing was wrong, the attendant stepped back into the hall and the door swung shut.

There was a flavor of wariness in Doctor Varn's approach toward Baynard Mulligan.

"Doctor, I would like you to brief Mr. McGee on the Doris Wrightson case."

"I don't believe that would be advisable," Varn said.

Mulligan ignored him. Looking at me, he said, "I can give you a layman's appraisal of her condition when she was brought in. She was a thirty-one-year-old spinster, shy, frail and introverted, an office worker in poor physical condition. Chronic migraine headaches, a susceptibility to infections of the urinary tract, pains in the lower back. Her pulse was rapid and irregular. Emotionally she was tense, anxious, with poor social and emotional adjustments. She became very upset when office routine was disturbed. Though she was a good worker, she tired easily, and she would weep when spoken to harshly. And she had the strange idea that she was sent here for treatment merely because she had stumbled across some irregularity in the accounting system and had come to me, snuffling and wringing her hands, to accuse our Mr. Penerra of peculation." He turned to Varn. "Certainly, Doctor, she had many physical and emotional problems?"

"Yes. Of course."

"But Doctor Varn is obviously reluctant to discuss the experimental treatment, even though it was astonishingly successful."

"I do not believe we should . . ."

"Experimentations along this line have been conducted in the USSR for some years, didn't you tell me, Doctor?"

"But . . ."

"Everything else that is done here, McGee, can be classified as acceptable therapy. But in this country we have such a sentimental approach to the value of the human animal, that if this line of inquiry became known, mobs would probably appear to burn this place to the ground. It makes Doctor Varn nervous. Please tell Mr. McGee how Doris Wrightson was treated, Doctor."

The two men stared at each other in silent conflict. I saw a gleam of sweat on Varn's bald head. Suddenly Varn gave a small shrug of acceptance. In a perfectly flat voice he said, "After a complete series of tests, an electrode in the form of a very fine alloy wire was inserted into that area of the patient's brain—that deep area which can loosely be defined as the pleasure area. Proper location was achieved through trial and error. A transistorized field-current setup was then adjusted as to the volume of the signal to give a maximum stimulus. In effect this resulted in an intensified pleasure sensation, a simultaneous experiencing of all pleasures, emotional and physical. The patient was given physical tasks, within the limits of her capacities, with the equipment set up in such a manner that the completion of the task would close a contact and give a ten-second stimulus. It was discovered that once the patient had been started on such a cycle, she would continue of her own volition until totally exhausted. Following these procedures, we have made detailed observations of muscle generation, the psychology and physiology of sleep, nutrition, the pleasure phenomenon and related matters."

"Could we see the patient, Doctor?" Mulligan said.

"She's resting now."

"Doctor, I can remain more convinced of the value of your programs here when I can be given a chance to observe results. Right now there is a list of equipment purchases on my desk for approval."

Varn went to the door and spoke to the man outside. Doris Wrightson was brought in a few minutes later. There was a scarf tied around her head. She wore a gray denim hospital dress that looked too small for her—loose at the waist, but tight across breasts and hips. She moved with a ponderous litheness—that odd gait of the perfectly-conditioned athlete. Musculature squared her jaw. Her shoulders and neck were solid and heavy, packing the fabric of the dress. In repose her arms and legs had the roundness and illusion of softness of a woman, but at the slightest move, the slabbed muscles distorted contour, as explicit as an anatomical drawing. For a moment I could not think what she reminded me of, and then I saw it. She was precisely like one of the circus girls: one of those hard, chunky, quiet, amiable fliers—narrow-waisted, flat-bellied—with thighs like a warmed layer of thin foam rubber stretched over granite, and with such pectoral development that even the high round breasts are muscular. This was no sedentary office worker, nor could I imagine her as ever having been one. She said, "Hello, Doctor. Hello, Mr. Mulligan," and then stood off to one side, placid and incurious as a good dog. Though she was very pale, her skin had the moist luminous glow of perfect health, and the whites of her mild brown eyes were blue-white.

Varn said, "She's now at the point where, with a rig designed on the basis of a rowing machine, she will expend forty-eight hundred foot pounds of energy a minute—fifty foot tons an hour—and maintain that rate for eight hours in two four-hour segments. It requires a five-thousand calory intake to keep her weight stabilized on that basis. As we keep increasing effort required, we alter the specific physical motions in order to avoid overdevelopment of any specific muscle areas."

"How do you feel, Doris?" Mulligan asked.

"I feel very good, thank you."

"All other physical problems have disappeared," Varn said. "Her normal heartbeat at rest is approximately fifty."

"Can you explain her emotional adjustment?"

"Only by inference," Varn said. "As you can see, she is placid and amiable and cooperative. Social interractions and interrelations no longer concern her. She is not anxious about how people react to her. She is totally unselfconscious. Her desire to please is based upon our ability to provide her with that pleasure stimulus which forms a compulsion so complete nothing else is of any particular concern to her. She takes pride in doing the hard tasks we set her, though, a pride a little apart from the reward of the pleasure stimulus."

"How about intelligence?" Mulligan asked.

"That's difficult. The conventions we use to measure intelligence are conditioned by emotional factors. The tests imply a wide range of emotional responses. She has one single emotional compulsion. My guess is that intelligence is unimpaired. But her indifference to anything other than the pleasure stimulus makes it difficult to measure. There seems to be an impairment of memory regarding everything which ever happened to her before she came here. Her skills seem unimpaired."

"What's your appraisal of the future?"

"I don't believe we're anywhere near the top limit of physical capability, even though her physical strength is astonishing right now. We're trying to keep her at that point of stasis where strength increases without any breakdown of muscle tissue. I would guess that the end point will be reached when the bone structure cannot take the stress involved."

"What will happen when you stop the experiment?"

"No!" Doris Wrightson cried, her face vivid with dismay.

Varn went quickly to her and said, "We're not going to stop, Doris. Don't be upset." He patted her shoulder. It was a gentling gesture, the way one pats the bulging shoulder of a nervous horse. She quieted quickly, less of the whites of her eyes showing, and he guided her to the door, turned her over to someone waiting there for her.

Varn came back and said, "That's the special problem, as

you can see. When we have tried stopping for one day, she becomes very restless and anxious and difficult to manage. It is, in a sense, a very strong addiction. But, unlike other addictions, there is no change in the tolerance level. The exact same percentage increase in the strength of the stimulus now will cause her to faint as it did in the beginning. There is the same effect from an increase in duration."

"What are you going to do with her?"

"We'll face that when we come to it, Mr. Mulligan. Dr. Moore has several suggestions. We'll try the least radical ones first."

"Would you be interested in another female?"

The quickening of interest on Varn's handsome face turned my heart to ice. "It improves the validity of any experimental procedure to have another subject to use as a control," he said. "But . . . we would want to be very certain that . . . there would be no one on the outside to insist on visiting . . ."

"Just like Miss Wrightson? I think I can guarantee that."

"Wilkerson is very interested in setting up an experiment for agility rather than strength. He has the idea of a plate which the subject would have to touch to close the contact, and then he could put it a little higher each day . . ."

His patient impersonal explanation was lost in the roar of blood in my ears. In a little cold white tall room in the back of my mind, my Nina, in gray denim, with a wire in her head, with all of her world and her life focused down to a single recurrent ecstasy—crouched and sprang, crouched and sprang . . .

Varn was gone. Mulligan studied me. "At a lunch counter, McGee, somebody can reach across her to get a paper napkin. It would be that simple. Moore's report says that you have a strong sexual-emotional attachment for the girl—a protective instinct, with a slight overtone of moralistic guilt. That last astonished me somewhat."

"You are a bastard, Mulligan."

"Dr. Varn's most bitter disappointment is that he cannot publish. But the fellow is endlessly curious. There are certain unpleasantly feral implications in turning people into hopelessly dependent compulsives, but who are we to say that a hundred years from now history might acclaim the good doctor as the one who found the way of turning man into superman. From a beginning of rewarding strength or agility, why not reward the problem-solving ability, or artistic effort, or mind-reading? Or maybe it will be a world where all the dutiful clods wear their little wires, and men of high intelligence and ambition push the buttons. Our bald little doctor is properly nervous about this field of investigation, but he is careful about his security measures. He is inquisitive, not monstrous. And I am not without compassion."

"You are a legitimate maniac, Mulligan. You are the one they should lock up."

"Don't be childish. Years ago, when I was looking for exactly the right angle of approach, I realized it would be stupid to try to contrive enough fatal accidents to take care of people who might get in the way of a long-range, large-scale project. This has worked well. After these people were bribed and coerced into their first illegal, unethical, unprofessional act, they've had no choice but to be cooperative. I don't acually give a damn about their rationalizations. Charlie was their first project, you are the sixth, Olan Harris is the seventh, and Miss Gibson can be the eighth. I think you will write the letters, McGee. I think you will make every effort to make them plausible and convincing. I do not think you will try to be clever or tricky. As soon as you have written them, you are no longer a problem to me, and I shall probably never see you again. I may see you after your personality has been surgically adjusted, and you will probably remember me and feel a sense of antagonism. But you won't be dangerous."

"I'll be a very happy man."

"That's everybody's goal, isn't it?"

"Let them treat *you*, Mulligan."

"I am a happy man, my friend. I'm getting my gratification from finding a way past all the rules and restrictions and conventions of a dull and orderly society. I'm performing a theft of such dimensions, it will be legend rather than theft. And, like our Doctor Varn, I am slightly bitter because I will never be able to publish the details of it. But books will be written about it. From the look of you, I think you are ready to write those letters."

I was, and I did.

eleven

I WAS WOVEN into delicious clouds, high and ecstatic on softened hilltops, taking the slow, sweet, aching suffusions of the warm slow drift of great masses of pure color, which moved across me and through me and changed in almost imperceptible ways. I was one, united to pure sensation, everything about me becoming a part of me, a fabulous unity, so that I knew at last the ultimate fact of all existence, knew it and knew that there were no words with which it could be expressed because it was beyond words. I rolled over and stretched my arms into a strange grass, more like hair than grass, metallic blue-green in color, springing out of the soft white earth-flesh; hair-grass thick as pencils, half as tall as a man, making a strange electric tingling wherever it touched my flesh. I rolled and saw leaning to me a golden reaching softness of limbs of ancient Martian trees—reaching, grasping gently, curling, caressing, taking me up and through brightness and then into a dusky feathery hollow between enormous breasts, into a stroking and fitting and long long gentle never-ending orgasm. . . .

Tiny bright light swinging and my voice in a darkened room.

Brush and soap and shower. "He was never worth a goddam until they moved him to linebacker."

Light in the room at night. Face at the grill in the door.

Pasty feel of electrodes at the temples, pen scratching a rhythmic line on a chart.

"Now, Travis, run in position until I tell you to stop."

Indifferent face in the night. Needle fang in my arm. Cool wipe of alcohol. Medicine smell. Off into drifting . . .

They wanted a manageable patient, a mild eagerness to cooperate. There were times when I felt I was fighting my way to the surface and then I would be pushed down again, down into the drifting. No problem to anybody. When I got close to the surface I would know that some terrible thing was going to happen, but I did not know what it was.

I do not know how they slipped up, or why they slipped up. Perhaps it was one of those little errors in routine, somebody skipping a medication indicated on the chart. But suddenly I came awake in the night. I did not know what night it was, or how much time had passed. I knew only that I was alert and terrified. Wisps of strange dreams and visions clotted the corners of my mind. The night light was sealed into the baseboard, guarded with a heavy grill. I looked out the door grill into a segment of empty gray corridor.

I paced the room, and, at the first rattle of the latch, got quickly into bed. It was the square sandy nurse. She fixed the hypo in the dim light. When she bared my arm and bent over it, I hit her sharply on the shelf of the jaw, near the chin. She fell across me without a sound. I found the hypo when I shifted her cautiously. I got up and straightened her out and looked in her pockets. I found the little vial from which she filled the hypo. I injected her in the arm with what was in the hypo, then drew off more from the vial, sticking the needle through the soft rubber top, and gave her that. She had a split ring with two keys on it. I did not know what they fitted. She had left my door wedged open a few inches. She was on the floor on her back. Her mouth hung open. She began to snore. I rolled her onto her face. She stopped snoring. I shoved her under the bed. She slid easily on the gray vinyl flooring. I was in the short hospital gown I wore at night. They would bring me clean coveralls each morning. The door to the tiled bath was locked. I did not dare go out into the hallway. This might be the only chance I would have. They would know how to handle patients who got out into the corridors. They would have safe, practical, effective methods. They would never give me a second chance. There would be nothing left but the dreams and visions until they had finished their series, and then there would be a tiny blade shoved into my head, and after that I would never worry very much about anything.

The room door opened inward. It was held open by a rubber wedge. I listened. I heard nothing. I pulled the door halfway open and wedged it. The night light made a fairly bright area just inside the door. I had to bait it with something. I used her keys. They caught the light. They would catch the eye of anyone passing. The normal reaction would be to pick them up. I waited alongside the door, where I could not be seen through the grill. I waited a long time. I heard someone coming. Scuff of a shoe. Faint rustle of clothing. I clenched my hands together. I heard a soft exclamation. The instant I saw a hand reaching for the keys, I jumped out and brought my clenched hands down on the nape of a neck, as hard as I could. He made too much noise tumbling onto the floor. I pulled him inside, wedged the door open an inch or so. I dragged him over beside the bed. I was going to inject him. But as I touched him, he gave a prolonged shudder and died. I worked his clothing off him and put it on. The legs and sleeves were short. I was worried about the shoes. I wanted shoes. But they were just big enough. I put him into the bed and covered him over. I felt in the pockets. There was a wallet. I took it to the light. He was Donald Swane. He had three keys. One of them was identical to one of the nurse's keys. I felt sorry for the poor dead son-of-a-bitch. He had no way of knowing that some of the patients didn't belong there. Which ones do you believe?

He had eleven dollars, half a pack of Camels, a Zippo lighter, three keys, half a roll of clove Life Savers, and no weapon at all. Once upon a time I had tried to memorize the layout of the building. I couldn't remember much of it.

I didn't want to walk out of the room. It seemed like a safe place. I didn't know what was waiting outside. His shoes were quiet. They had rubber soles. I carried the hypo and vial in the pocket of the white jacket. I opened the door and looked up and down the corridor. It was empty. To my left I saw a red bulb burning over a doorway. I remembered there were stairs there. I walked swiftly, letting the door close behind me. I went through the stairway door. I had left his watch on his wrist. It was after four in the morning. I wanted to go down the stairs. As I started to go down, a door opened on the next flight down, and somebody started coming up. I went up. There was only one more flight. I waited until I was certain they were coming all the way up. I went out into a corridor very like the one on my floor below. I pulled a door open. It was a lab. A blue night light shone on tubing and retorts, zinc benches, bottle racks. I made certain the door could be opened from the inside, and let it shut. I crouched against the door, straining my ears to hear any sound in the corridor. The door was too thick. I waited at least five minutes. Then I looked around the lab. The windows were steel casement windows, rigidly braced. They did not open far enough for me to get out. I was on the third floor. I could have risked a drop from that height.

I wanted a weapon. I searched the small lab. I found a short heavy length of pipe. I tied it into a towel. I looked into a big refrigerator. It was full of racks of small vials containing colorless fluid. They were marked in a D series. D-1 to D-17. Many of them had sub-numerals in parentheses. I took vials of D-15, three of them, and some of the other numbers. They were small. I had the idea that if I could get out of there, the vials would be some proof of what was being done there, provided they were the Daska compounds. Somehow I saw all the doctors I had not met as looking exactly like Varn, all handsome little bald fellows.

It felt reassuring to have a club in my hand. I expected alarm bells to go off at any moment. I thought they would have some way of sounding an alarm when a patient was loose. Perhaps a siren. The corridor was empty. I ran to the stairs and went racing down. I got down to the ground floor level. The corridor there was much wider. I remembered a time, a lifetime ago, when I had been taken down to talk to Baynard Mulligan. It seemed a longer corridor than the ones upstairs. In the far distance I saw two nurses standing and talking. If I could not see their faces, they could not see mine. There had to be an exit in that direction, perhaps halfway between me and the nurses. I walked toward them, trying to move casually. Suddenly a man came out of a doorway forty feet in front of me and started walking toward me, looking at a piece of paper he held in his hand.

I pushed open the first door I came to and went in. I was in a kitchen area. Two men were working slowly and sleepily at a big range. A dull-looking girl stood at a work table yawning and slicing grapefruit into halves. There was a lot of stainless steel and steam racks. They all looked at me questioningly.

"You seen Don?" I asked.

"What the hell would he be doing in here? Go look in the dining room."

There was a long passthrough area at one end of the room. I could look through there into a big institutional dining area. I saw the swinging doors with push plates which had to lead there. I walked toward the doors.

"Don who?" the girl asked.

"Skip it."

The dining area was empty. There was a long counter with low stools and beyond it, a cafeteria area adjacent to the passthrough. A busty redheaded girl in a blue nylon uniform stood at the work area behind the counter, slicing small boxes of dry cereal and placing the boxes into white bowls.

She glanced at me and said, "You want coffee, it's about

115

three more minutes. I threw out the old, it tasted like battery acid, man." She gestured toward a huge gleaming urn that stood on the counter.

As I started to turn away, she said, "You new?"

"Brand new."

"Didn't take you long to get the coffee habit. It's like my husband says it's that way in the navy."

Find a door and walk out, I thought. And then what? Are there walls, gates, guards? Is it way out in the country? Any way to get a car?

"Rest yourself while you wait, man."

I needed a diversion. I needed everybody looking in some other direction. I sat on a stool. The vials in my pocket clinked. I stared at the long distortion of my face in the shining urn. Why the hell not?

"Mind if I look in the top of that thing?"

"What for? You look at those tube things and you can tell, it's when they get dark enough."

"I was wondering how they make them now," I said. I got up onto the counter and pulled the lid.

"Hey!" she said.

"This is very interesting."

"Climb in and have a swim. You a nut or something."

She turned back to her cereal. I thumbed the rubber tops off the vials of D compound and dumped them in. Maybe they were harmless. Maybe they were cholera germs. Maybe heat changed them. It was too late to wonder about it. Scores slain in coffee poisoning. I wiped the counter with a paper napkin. I sat on a stool. She looked at me and her face was losing form, sliding and loosening like melting candy. I heard a strange prolonged chord of music in a minor key. The walls of the big room tilted inward toward me, and the edges of reality had turned pink.

"You feel okay?" she asked, out of a mouth that was sliding down her throat into the top of her uniform.

"Just a little residual hallucination."

"Huh? Oh."

"I'll be back for some of your delicious coffee, angel."

"You do that."

"Don't melt while I'm gone."

"Melt? It isn't hot in here, man."

The door kept receding as I walked toward it. It took me three or four hours to reach it. I went into the corridor. I found a storage room. I folded myself into a cement corner behind huge cartons of toilet paper, and held my fists against

116

my eyes and tried to keep the whole world from melting away into a pink eternal nothing. In seven or eight months the world began to refocus and solidify. The musical chord died away, and I could hear clattering, shouts, a bell ringing. I got up and walked out into a vast confusion. I heard glass breaking. Two men were trying to hold a third man. He was screaming, spasming, throwing them all over the corridor. I edged by them. A woman stood braced with her back against the wall, eyes closed, expression dreamy, slowly driving her nails into her cheeks and yanking them out again, blood running onto her beige blouse. I walked by her. I reached the main entrance. The world was out there, beyond tall glass, a bright cool morning. A man on all fours was in a corner, trying to ram his way through, backing up and lunging forward like a big stubborn turtle trapped in a box. A girl sat spraddled on the floor. Her blouse was ripped to rags. Her empty eyes looked at me. She was sucking her thumb and slowly massaging her small loose breasts.

A man lay quite still just outside the main doors. I stepped over him. I heard sirens. I saw ambulances. People were running toward the building. They ignored me. I saw the parking lot and walked steadily toward it.

Off to my right I saw a fat woman running in a big circle as though she were running an imaginary base path. A big car came into the lot just as I got there. A man slammed the brakes on and piled out. "What the *hell* is going on?" he demanded. "What's happening in there?"

I turned him around and rapped him behind the ear with my length of pipe. When he fell, his car keys spilled out of his hand. I peeled his topcoat off and put it on. I took his car and drove away from there. Fifteen minutes later I was on the Thruway, heading south toward the city. Twenty minutes later the sides of the highway began to curl upward and turn pink and the musical sound began again. I had to pull off. It took twenty minutes to get from my lane to the shoulder. The car was barely moving. But when it reached the shoulder it began to leap up and down. I stopped it short of a tree and lay down on the seat with my arms wrapped around my head. My own face was melting off. I could feel it. I could hear it drip onto the seat upholstery.

Several months later the world resolidified and I drove on.

I drove down off the parkway at Forty-sixth. I drove over Forty-fourth and abandoned the car a couple of blocks short of Times Square. I walked south and found a sleazy hotel and paid five-fifty for a small sour room. I stretched out on

117

the bed, still in the stolen topcoat, and waited for the edges of everything to start to turn pink again. I had noticed the clock in the lobby. It was quarter after ten. I wondered what year it was.

twelve

WE ARE supposed to learn from our mistakes. I had walked into the Armister situation with all the jaunty confidence of a myopic mouse looking for a piece of cheese in the cobra cage.

But by the narrowest margin possible I had escaped spending the rest of my life as a very happy fellow working, perhaps, in a shoe factory over in Jersey.

I had to make some kind of a move now, but everything I could think of scared me. The Mulligan group had all kinds of weight and pressure. I was an escaped nut. A demonstrably murderous nut. And I had no proof of anything.

Charlie was my walking proof. Charlie was my boy. But I didn't see how I could get to within a thousand yards of him.

But maybe somebody else could, if they knew enough.

Like a loving wife?

I picked my phone up. A thin and adenoidal voice said, "You wanna make any outside calls, you got to leave the money at the desk. Twenny cents each, local calls."

I found my apprehensive way down and left a dollar and got back to safe refuge. Then I realized how stupid I was being. I had made all the mistakes I was permitted. I rubbed cold water on my face and studied my mirror image. The eyes looked strange. With the topcoat buttoned, the white jacket did not show. I had a crust of one-day beard. Noticeable, but not too bad.

I went down again and got change for my dollar and found the phone booths in the dim back of the stale lobby.

I tried the Plaza. Mrs. Drummond was not registered. They gave me a forwarding address in Athens.

I leaned against the phone for a little while. I got information. She looked up the Long Island number for Mr. Charles

Armister, told me how to dial it and how much to feed the coin slots.

I got a soft-voiced woman with a pronounced accent. She told me Mrs. Armister was in the city. At the apartment. She gave me the phone number. I checked the book. It was the number listed for the other apartment, the one further uptown.

I dialed that one. Terry Drummond answered. That brassy sardonic voice was one of the world's better sounds.

"McGee! They bought you off, obviously. What's the matter, ducks? You want to see if you can get a better price from me? How'd you find me?"

"Nobody bought me off."

"Sweetie, it was perfectly obvious to me from your note that . . ."

"Shut up! I have something important to tell you, Terry. I don't know how much time I have. I wasn't bought off. They had me in a mental hospital."

"In a what?"

"Get a pencil and paper so you can write things down. I don't know how long I can last. I'll try to give you the cold facts."

"Hold on just a minute, Trav."

I waited. A softer voice came on the line and gave a cautious, "Hello?"

It had a little of the quality of Terry's voice, but was far more subdued.

"Trav? Joanna is on the extension."

"This isn't the sort of thing she should hear, Terry."

"If it has anything to do with my husband, I want to hear it," Mrs. Armister said firmly.

"All right. I don't know how you can check these things out, but if you get good lawyers and get the authorities in on it, maybe you can move. Baynard Mulligan heads up a group which has stolen six million dollars so far from Charles Armister. There are nine of them. Mulligan, Penerra and Bonita Hersch, those are the only names I know. They plan to work at it for another eighteen months and build it up to twenty million and then skip. When anybody gets troublesome, they get put in the Mental Research Wing of the Toll Valley Hospital up across the river from Poughkeepsie. Write these things down. They've got people up there now who got in the way. Olan Harris, who was the chauffeur. A secretary named Doris Wrightson. And others whose names I don't know. They get them legally committed. They did that to me too. I escaped this morning. I killed a man getting out of there."

"Dear God," Terry rumbled.

"That's where Charles went when he . . ."

"Shut up, Joanna," Terry said.

"When Charlie was up there," I said, "they operated on him. They stuck a knife in his head. I think it's called a lobotomy. That made him easy to manage. They keep him happy, and he signs anything. But anybody who didn't know him before would think he was perfectly all right."

I heard a soft, weak, wailing cry of despair and Terry said sharply, "Pull yourself together, Jo!"

"Write down these names of doctors. God knows where they came from, or how they ever got licenses. Mulligan has them in the palm of his hand. He supports the experimental program. Varn, Moore, Daska and Wilkerson. And listen. Don't go flying off in all directions. There's a hell of a mess out there right now, but if they can get it quieted down fast enough, and if you get in the way, you both could end up out there with little wires in your heads, and electric currents making you jump around like monkeys on a stick."

"Can this be true?" Joanna wailed.

"Sister, dear, I will vouch for McGee. He is a very rough type, and he sounds angry, and what he says explains a lot of very curious things. McGee, where are you? Can I help you? What do you need?"

"Money."

"Sweetie, I have the thousand dollars I was going to use to bribe that tart who never showed up. Will that help?"

"A lot. But get moving on this other stuff first. Listen. This is important for both of you. Don't eat out. Don't drink anything anywhere. Fix your own food and drink right there and don't let anybody near it. Don't even let anybody buy it for you."

"But why?"

"One drop of a tasteless, odorless substance can turn you into something they come after with a net. They worked it on me, maybe on Charlie and probably on the others. It imitates insanity."

"Sweetie, this is priceless. I used to adore Fu Man Chu."

"You have a great sense of humor, Terry. You are as funny as a crutch."

"I'm sorry, Trav. It's just my image speaking."

"By now Mulligan knows I'm loose, I would imagine. He is going to be very anxious to find me and shut my mouth.

And he can afford a lot of help. I need money, and then I need a place to go, a place for two people to go, if I can . . ."

"Sweetie, where are you?"

I drew such a blank I had to look at the tag on my room key. "The Harbon Hotel on West 41st. Room 303."

"You wait right there," she said and hung up.

But I was in a horrid haste to find the next number and fumble the next dime into the slot. I had thought the best thing to do would be to protect Nina by staying out of touch with her. But in telling Terry what Mulligan might do, I had realized Nina was the best possible weapon for him to use against me. He had proved that point once.

The cool British accent of the receptionist was an implacable barrier. She was teddibly sorry, Miss Gibson was in conference and could not be disturbed. I said it was life and death. She said that if I would leave my name and number, she would have Miss Gibson call me. I cursed her and she sighed and broke the connection. With my last dime I called back. With great gentleness I stressed the urgency of the situation. I begged her to have Miss Gibson phone Mr. Jones in Room 303 at the Harbon Hotel as soon as possible. I stressed the room number. I was certain the place was full of Joneses, miss and mister.

I bought a paper. The stairs tilted sideways. The railing felt like a wet snake. I shoved seven keys at seven keyholes and they all fitted and all turned, and I stumbled into a pink room and curled up on the bed, my knees against my chest. As I fought it, I thought with a sickening remorse of the people out there at Toll Valley—the man butting his head into a corner, the woman pulling bits of meat out of her face, the thumb sucker, the base runner—all of them so ruthlessly tumbled into that horrible place where reality was warped, where things came out of the wall. They were all innocents. They could not know that the private hospital was being used in a vicious way. They were staff, visitors, ambulatory patients—anybody entitled to go into the dining room and have a cup of nightmare.

It dwindled away. All the pink unstable edges turned back to normal hue and I straightened myself out, in post-hallucination depression. For the ultimate in depressive experiences, try a little jolt of induced insanity while wearing a dead man's clothing in a cheap hotel room. Cold air-shaft light came into the room, shining on the dusty sour rug, on a blonde bureau with missing knobs, on places on the headboard of the bed where brown paint had been chipped and gouged away. Ten thousand people had left a stink of loneliness in this room. Here they had paced, coughed, snapped their knuckle bones, spilled their drinks, taken their pills, belched, sighed, wept, scratched, dreamed, vomited, smoked, bragged, cursed and groaned. In this room each had endured his or her own special kind of sickness, felt despair, and either accepted or inflicted something they called love.

I saw the paper where I had dropped it, just inside the door. I went over and got it and took it back to the bed. While I had been in the blurry world of induced dreams and visions, the other world had trudged its way along to a November Tuesday. Education bill returned to committee. Three injured in Birmingham bomb attack. Actress beats narcotics rap. Seven dead in Freeway collision. Park lands sold to campaign contributor. Truck strike in eighth week. Thirty-nine dead in jet crash. Model claims fractured jaw in divorce action. Disarmament talks stalled. Teacher accused of teen slayings. Earthquake in Peru. Launching failure. Tax cut stymied . . .

. . . I was back in the sane, reasonable, plausible world.

Terry Drummond rapped at my door and I let her in. She wore fifteen thousand dollars worth of glossy fur coat. Her brown simian face wrinkled with distaste as she looked around. "God, what a scrimey hole!" The coat swung open. The body of eternal girl was clad in gray slacks and a wine-red cardigan. She stared at me. "And you look worn around the edges, dear. And thinner. And where did you get that grim grubby clothing?"

"Off the boy I had to kill to get out of there."

She swallowed and sat down quickly. "You do get damned explicit. Maybe I'm not as used to the facts of life as I thought I was. But we did hear Toll Valley Hospital very prominently mentioned over the noon news broadcast."

"What did they say?"

"Something about mysterious poisoning, four dead in violent and unpleasant ways, and dozens injured, and dozens out of their mind, patients escaping and so on; and apparently the first batch of people who got there to quiet things down suddenly began to go just as mad as the rest of them. They said something about experimental drugs getting out of hand. It seems that there is still a state of horrible confusion up there, and all kinds of investigations being started, and experts roaring in from all over, and reporters and police and television and everything. Did you do all that, darling boy?"

123

I did not answer. Four dead. Four innocents.

"Trav?" she said in the softest voice I had ever heard her use.

I lifted my head and looked at her.

"Please don't look so terribly agonized. You did what you had to do. I'm sure of that. I've started things going. I believe what you said about them doing something terrible to Charlie out at that place. From the news report, it sounds as if you managed to destroy it. I'm not going to let anything happen to you on account of that, believe me. They were giving you drugs, weren't they?"

"They were giving me drugs."

"Then you cannot be held responsible. Which is worse, Trav, some deaths and injuries, or that place going on and on . . . *doing* things to people?"

"I can devise my own rationalizations, thanks."

"Don't be cold and cruel. Sweetie, I brought the money, but after I got Joanna calmed down, we had another idea. You want a safe place for two people? The other one would be your little Gibson girl you told me about? My dear Roger King is alerting all the legal troops. I am certain he can erect some sort of protective throng around the apartment at East Seventy-ninth. It's really quite vast, and Joanna brought in some of the staff from the Island. I don't think we'd need extra protection, but it would probably make you happier. So let's go on back to the apartment, and then I can go gather up your little friend, and we can all sit there and plan the utter destruction of creepy Baynard."

"How did you get here?"

"By taxi. He's sitting down there with his meter clicking."

"You just walked out of the apartment and took a cab."

"Of course," she said blankly.

"And nobody followed you?"

"My word, aren't we getting a bit paranoiac?"

My phone rang.

"Hello?"

"Trav! Oh, Trav, darling, thank God!"

"That letter I wrote you . . ."

"Was the most complete nonsense ever written. It was a cry for help. I was going out of my mind with worry. The moment I got it I went at once to . . ."

"We better do our talking later. Do exactly as I say, Nina. It's very important. Get out of there as soon as you can. If there is any kind of back exit or side exit, use it."

"But . . ."

"That place where we went, near your office, that first day. Go there. Wait for me there. Don't have a drink. Just wait for me. Don't talk to anybody. Just wait there alone."

"Trav, I . . ."

"Please!"

She agreed. I hung up, and turned and looked at Terry Drummond. Her odd-green eyes looked damp. "It's important with that one?"

"Very."

"That makes me feel such a wistful old bag, ducks. Hold me a minute? I have a case of the horrors."

She came to me. I put my arms around the resiliency, the warmth of girl under that fur coat and held her close. She tucked her brown puckered face into my neck and sighed.

"Well, hell," she said. "Let's go. Let's go pick up your young stuff and run for cover."

I shoved the sheaf of large bills into the wallet of the dead Donald Swane. I said, "We are going to cheat your cabby, Terry."

"We can't. I gave him a ten to hold him there. But I'll play your games, dear. We sneak out another way?"

"If you can bear it."

"I can."

"Terry, every once in a while I go off. I hallucinate. I have to fold. I don't know how long it lasts. But don't be scared. I come out of it. It seems to be a little bit less each time. If it happens in public, just keep people away from me and give me time to come out of it."

Her mouth looked pale. "All right, Trav."

There was no other way to leave. We went out the main entrance and turned away from the waiting cab. That coat was too damned conspicuous. "Lady! Hey, lady!" We walked swiftly to the corner.

The panting driver caught up to us. "Hey, lady! You coming back to the cab?"

"Keep the change, my good man."

"But that guy is waiting for you in the cab."

"What guy?" she demanded.

"The one come out of the hotel after you went in, the one you told he should wait in my cab, lady."

He turned and pointed. We looked. A man was walking diagonally across 41st, heading in the opposite direction, moving swiftly.

"Hey, there he goes!" the driver said.

I grabbed Terry's arm and hustled her around the corner

125

and walked her as fast as she could go. "Hey!" she said. "Hey, I apologize. For everything."

At the next corner I saw a cab discharging passengers. I ran her over to it and we piled in. He pulled his flag down. I said, "Make some turns here and there, driver. A very busy process server is trying to hand the lady a paper."

He started up and said, "You looked in a hurry. But the way I see it, what's the use? Sooner or later you get nailed."

"I'd like to make it later," Terry said.

The driver was good. He judged the lights so as to be the last car around each corner as the light changed. He angled crosstown and downtown, and said, "Unless he rented a whirlybird, friend, he's nowhere."

I gave him the block on Park I wanted. Terry said in a low voice, "I never saw that man before in my life. What was he going to do to me?"

I made a grim joke. "Process you," I said. She put her hand on her throat. "And they'll have to process Charlie too. If he's dead, nobody can prove what was done to him. Nobody can test him."

Her eyes looked like green glass. "You can't be serious."

"He's part of the proof."

She waited in the cab. I went in to get Nina. She was on the left of the entrance. There was a man sitting on either side of her. She looked pale and strained. The two men looked deft and deadly and competent. I paused. The men's trim shaven faces began to turn into bristly dog faces, dogs in dark suits, in pink light, with a white kitten between them. Dimly I realized that it was emotional stress which was bringing this on, time after time. I could curl up on the floor and hold my fists against my eyes. I staggered, and launched myself through the pink light, straining toward the nearest dog, yelling to Nina in a great cracked, croaking voice, "Run! Run!" I could give her that much. She had not asked for any part of this. I didn't want her in gray denim with wires in her head. I would rather be eaten by the dogs.

I caught a dog throat, hurled a dog body wide and far, whirled in pinkness to dive past the kitten, was cracked, and foundered, and was dwindled down to black flow, to a dark puddled sinking nothing. . . .

thirteen

I AWOKE naked between crisp sheets in a big shadowy bedroom. There was a lamp with a blue shade in a far corner. The blue light made little gleamings of richness on the corners and edges of things. I could hear a faint whisper of night traffic. I turned my head slowly. A far door was ajar. There was a brighter light beyond it. My head felt strange. I lifted my hand and touched my head and felt gauze and tape.

I wondered if I was now a very happy fellow. This would be the lion's den, of course. The quiet and spacious luxury of the inner sanctum, where Mulligan and Hersch kept a pet named Charlie Armister. Marvelous talent for organization.

I lay and wondered how happy I was. How uninhibited. Maybe Mulligan could use me as chauffeur, replacing the greedy and unreliable Harris. But a job like that would require initiative. I would need supervision. Maybe they had gathered us all up and made us all very happy. Terry and Joanna. And Nina.

Then I knew I was not happy at all. I could remember every fraction of every instant with her, every kiss and contour.

No matter what the bastards did, McGee would keep trying. He would keep on clattering on in there, banging the rusty armor, spurring the spavined old steed, waving the mad crooked lance. I rolled up and sat on the edge of the bed. The rug was thick and soft against bare feet. I could see a dressing table, a faint gleam of bottles and jars aligned against the mirrors. I saw a small white fireplace, stood up, swayed for a moment and tottered over to it. There was a rack of shiny fireplace tools. Brass. I selected the poker. As I turned, I saw myself in a mirrored door. Big brown spook with a surgical turban. I tottered and brandished my weapon and whispered, "Tally ho."

127

I prowled silently to the door that was ajar. It was a bathroom done in pink, gold and white. It was empty. I wrapped a big towel around my waist and knotted it. I went back through the bedroom and put my ear against the closed door. I could hear a low distant murmur of voices. I opened the door cautiously. It opened onto a dim carpeted hallway. At the end of the hallway was a living room. I could see a segment of it, a drift of smoke, a tailored male shoulder. Several men seemed to be talking at once. Plotting. I heard the rattle of ice in a glass.

The hell with them. I would burst among them and see how many skulls I could crack before they wore me out. I took the brass poker in both hands. I took a deep breath. I headed for that big room, and just as I got there, I let out the war cry of a thousand disreputable years of McGees. As I yelled, the towel knot came undone. The towel slipped and wrapped around my ankles. I plunged free and went stumbling across the room in wild, head-down run. I ran into the glass doors of a huge breakfront desk loaded with porcelains, crashed, rebounded, cracked myself across the mouth with the handle of the poker, lay dazed and sprawling and looked up into the frozen astonishment on the faces of a dozen men, and on the face of Terry Drummond, and on the face of Nina Gibson, and on the old, worn, dignified face of Constance Trimble Thatcher.

"Whose apartment *is* this?" I managed to ask in a humble voice.

The man in charge sat by my bed and gave small guarded explanations. He did not want to say anything he did not have to say. His name was Beggs. His face was almost entirely nose, with a little mouth tucked under the bottom edge of it, and little eyes crowded up against each side of it.

"We had been making a quiet investigation for some time," he said.

"Who is we?"

"A cooperative venture between interested agencies. Certain small irregularities came to our attention. When Miss Gibson went to the Bureau with your letter, they turned her over to us and she told us what she knew. It . . . uh . . . became a matter of greater urgency. We decided she should have protection at all times. The two men with her were the two you assaulted."

"How did I do?"

"Splendidly, until you fell and hit your head on the edge

of the table. Mrs. Drummond insisted you be brought here."

"Now what?"

"What do you mean?"

"What are you doing about all this great urgency?"

"Everything is going reasonably well."

"Don't I have the right to know what's going on?"

"What right? For blundering around endangering people?"

"The inherent, God-given right of every total damned fool, Mr. Beggs."

A little smile curled in the deep shadow of the nose.

"What particularly concerns you?"

"What about Charlie?"

"You do have rather a nice instinct for these things. Mrs. Drummond conveyed to me your fears about Mr. Armister, and so we dated our blank warrants and went in two hours ago. We had to break in. There was a suicide note, in his handwriting, beside him, and an empty bottle which had contained sleeping pills. There was no one else there. They pumped him out and gave him stimulants and began walking him. He's quite confused about what happened. He is at the hospital now. His wife is with him."

"What about Mulligan?"

"We believe we will locate him."

"And Bonita Hersch."

"Apparently Miss Hersch and Mr. Penerra are in the company of Mr. Mulligan. We have two other men in custody, and they seem to have the feeling that the others ran out on them. They may give us some excellent suggestions as to where to look. We believe that Mulligan and company delayed a little too long before trying to leave. Overconfidence, probably."

I hesitated before asking the next question. "Toll Valley?"

"What about it?"

"Is it out of business?"

"Hardly. It is a perfectly reliable place. But their Mental Research Wing has been closed down, and all staff persons, those who are well enough at the moment, charged with illegal practices, administering unauthorized medicines, performing unnecessary operations—that sort of thing. I imagine it will be a very lengthy investigation, and public interest may well die down before it is settled one way or another."

"Doctor Varn?"

"Killed himself at two o'clock this afternoon."

"There were some other people out there . . ."

He took out a small black pocket notebook. "Olan Harris,

129

George Raub, John Benjamin and Doris Wrightson. Yes. They have been moved to other institutions for intensive care. They were all employed by Armister interests in one way or another. I'm in hopes they can be made well enough to testify. If you have no other questions . . ."

"What about what happened out there?"

The little eyes sighted along that nose. They were as unreadable as raisins. "Apparently there was some sort of mixup where experimental compounds were accidentally used in their commissary department. There was such confusion I doubt if we will every know exactly what happened. It is even possible that Doctor Varn did it purposely, on an experimental basis."

"There were deaths?"

"Four. One was apparently from heart disease. One fell into a fountain and drowned. One woman stabbed herself with a serving fork. And an attendant apparently died of a fall."

"Is there any record of . . . my escaping from out there?"

"I don't know what you are talking about. There is no record of your ever having been out there, Mr. McGee. Mrs. Thatcher, who is, by the way, an old friend, assures me that there would certainly never be any reason for you to have been sent to such a place. She thinks you are unstable, but not in any particularly mental way."

"Testimony?"

"From you, Mr. McGee? I think not. I think we can struggle along without you. When we organize these matters, we like to be able to call upon witnesses who will stay within the areas we propose to prosecute."

It puzzled me for a moment, and then I said, "Oh! Charlie."

He nodded his approval. "Of course. What purpose would be gained? We will have enough without that. We don't seek sensational press coverage in these matters. The courts will appoint trustees to make audits and sort everything out and manage the money henceforth. And we do expect that some recovery of monies will be made. If we can lay hands on Mr. Mulligan, I expect he will be glad to arbitrate the matter."

"He should be gutted and broiled."

"You are very savage, but I imagine that disbarment, poverty and total anonymity will be a far more galling fate for Mr. Mulligan."

Someone knocked on the door. Beggs went to the door. He spoke in low tones to someone for a little while and then came back and stood beside my bed. "We expect to take

130

Penerra off a Mexico City flight when it stops in Houston. And Canadian authorities have the Hersch woman. Apparently Mulligan tricked her and abandoned her in Montreal."

"How about Mulligan?"

"She may have some useful information for the man I am sending up there. The report says she is very upset."

"What do you want of me?"

"Mr. McGee, we would all take it as a great favor to everyone concerned if you would gather your strength and go back to Florida where you came from, and keep your mouth shut. As a matter of fact, if you do not keep your mouth shut, I will subpoena you for every single court action arising from this whole mess, and it may take from three to five years to clean up, and I shall call you every time and let you sit and listen to what my people have to listen to, year after year. I assure you, Mr. McGee, that no one has ever made a more dreadful threat to you, or meant it more sincerely."

He smiled, swiveled the bulk of his nose around, and followed it out of the bedroom.

Terry came in and talked. Nina came in and talked. Servants brought dinner on a tray. Terry brought wine. Terry and Nina and I talked. The doctor came back and looked me over. He wanted to know what had happened to my mouth. Terry told him I had engaged in mortal combat with a breakfront desk. And lost. He looked at her with great suspicion, and told me I was ridiculously, impossibly, grotesquely healthy. But to get a lot of rest. He left pills, very small lavender ones. I took two. I washed them down with wine. Terry talked. Nina talked. I began to yawn. . . .

In the stilly depths of night and sleep, came a perfumed silken sliding, a warmth, a closeness and cautious caress. "Nina?" I said.

"Yes darling," she whispered.

A slow writhing luxurious warmth under shortie wisp of sheerness. Head tucked into my neck. A long slow arousing, coming from the pill-sleep into the needs of love. It was a sweet hypnosis, without haste. When she was shudderingly readied, and I was turning her to take her, too many little things added up to an almost subliminal wrongness. Something about the scents of her, something about lengths and textures, something about a less springy feel of her hair against my cheek, something about the way she avoided kissings, something about the deep sweep of curves which did not seem

131

right to my hands, even something about the catch of her breath in response. I stopped and pinned her and ran my hand over her hair and her face. My fingertips felt the soft little serrations on her face.

"Terry!" I whispered.

She hitched herself at me frantically. "Nevermind," she said in a gritty whisper. "It's way too late now. Do it. Come on, damn you!" And she tried in a convulsive grasping to join us. I broke her arms and legs away from me, and struggled away from her and stood up and went over to the other side of the room and sat, trembling, on the bench of the dressing table.

I sat and listened to all the foul growling words she could think of to call me. She raved her low-voiced threats. "Jo was going to be generous, and I'll make sure you won't get a dime. And I'll tell that cheap busty little girl of yours that you laid me. Who the hell do you think you are?"

"Are you through?"

"God, what a priss you are. You don't deserve an honest-to-God woman. Little shop girls. That's your speed, McGee. You can be a big hero to them. Come back here and prove you're a man."

"Are you through!"

She did not answer. I saw a pale stirring, and then the shape of her, indistinct, sitting on the edge of the bed. In her normal wry mocking tone she said, "Hell, I guess it was worth a try."

"I'm sorry, Terry."

"Am I that repulsive to you?"

"You know better than that."

"Then, just between friends, what put you off?"

"After I knew it was you?"

"After you knew it was me."

"When I knew it was you, I knew it wasn't Nina. That's about the only answer I can give you."

After a silence she said, "I guess that's the only answer there is. In some nutty way I guess I have to admire you. You are a strange animal, McGee. I'm not used to your kind. I don't think I've ever bedded another man who could have quit right then and there."

"It wasn't exactly easy."

"Thank you, ducks. That's some help. But, you know, you have left me in one hell of a condition."

"Go take a cold shower."

"There's romance for you. Well, I got tricky, and it didn't work, and I have only myself to blame."

I saw paleness move toward the door. She stopped at the door and said, "I hereby accuse you of probably being a pretty good man."

"Thank you."

"And I am not a very nice woman."

"You are probably nicer than you are willing to admit, Teresa."

"Ho, ho, ho," she said and went out and the latch clicked as she quietly closed the door.

I went back to the bed. It was scented with her. My heart was still running a little fast. I laughed at myself silently. Mocking and derisive. I had defended my honor. Righteous prig. I knew what I should have done. Once I had suspected who it really was, kept my damned mouth shut. Saved astonishment until later. How many times do you find yourself in bed with a legend? The three unholy McGees—the one I try not to be, and the one I wish I was, and the one I really am. Going ahead with it would have been the one I guess I try not to be. But sometimes I wish there was less clown in the one I really am. I go about getting walloped with bladders, and setting my own nose on fire. Maybe I want to be a true hero. But whenever I hear that word, the only hero I can think of is Nelson Eddy, yelling into Jeanette's face. And wearing his Yogi Bear hat.

While considering a cold shower for myself, I dropped back into sleep.

fourteen

THOUGH THEIR doctor lauded my health, I was not too content with it. The head wound was not too bad. I had hit the formica edge a slashing glancing blow across the hairline in front, and a four-inch flap of scalp had had to be stitched back into position. A few days later I acquired a pair of black eyes of such a deep hue and generous area that I resembled a large uneasy raccoon.

It wasn't physical damage which bothered me. It was psychic damage. We are all in a state of precarious balance, and it is difficult to realize how delicate that balance is until it is upset—either by emotions or clever chemistry. You do not quite trust all the perfectly reliable messages of the senses.

I found that I had a bigger emotional swing than I wanted. I would become vastly elated for no reason, and deeply depressed without warning. And sometimes I felt ludicrously close to girlish tears. The governer was out of kilter. I told myself I could not go about reacting like a Smith College sophomore, but I could not shake the feeling of emotional convalescence, of not being entirely certain of what I might do next. Though I stopped hallucinating, the world had lost its stability. It would give a vivid little hitch from time to time, like a brief cosmic hiccup.

I met Charles McKewn Armister and his wife. They were similar physical types—stocky, sandy, fit, outdoor people. Her attitude toward him was gentle and loving, protective and slightly apprehensive. They had employed a husky male chauffeur-nurse-valet-attendant to stay close to him and keep him out of mischief. Had I not known about him, I would have thought him a perfectly normal club-man bore. He had hearty and trivial conversation. He seemed in perpetual good spirits.

He pumped my hand and said, "We're indebted to you.

Yes sir. Pretty ugly mess. Knew old Bay for years. Never thought he'd try any hanky panky. Got some good chaps running the show now. Reliable. Like Jo says, it's time for me to relax and enjoy myself. Travel, do some sailing, sharpen up the old tennis, hey old girl?" He put his arm around his wife's waist, gave her a hearty hug, slid his freckled hand down to her matronly rear and gave her such a massive pinch she leapt into the air, eyes bulging.

"Charles!" she said. He laughed heartily.

He looked at me, smiling, and said, "They won't let me take a drink. Imagine that? They say I get too noisy. Matter of fact, I don't miss it. A man doesn't have to drink to feel good, does he?"

"Charles?"

"What, my dear? What?"

She looked at him with the loving earnest patience of a mother coaching a child. "Weren't you going to ask Mr. McGee something?"

"What? Oh yes, of course. Why don't you and little what's-her-name come stay with us for a bit out at the Island? Rest and recuperation, fellow. And recreation. Glad to have you. Indebted to you."

And with the smiling, absent-minded unconcern of any minor league outfielder, he reached his hand to the front of his beautifully tailored trousers and scratched his crotch.

"Uh. Thank you very much. But Miss Gibson and I are going down to North Carolina to see her brother. Perhaps some other time."

"Any time at all, fellow. Give us a ring any time."

"Charles, dear," Joanna said, "would you like to do down with Wade now and wait for me in the car?"

"What? Of course, old girl. Certainly."

Terry said, "I'll be out day after tomorrow to stay a few days, Charlie." She stepped to him to kiss him on the cheek. He chuckled, and before she could evade him, put his hands on her breasts and gave them a simultaneous squeeze like a clown honking a pair of rubber horns, and, still chuckling, went out through the door Wade was holding for him. The moment they were gone, the sisters flew into each other's arms, and clung and wept, making their small soft sisterly sounds. I went to the windows and stood with my back to them, heard murmurous mutual comfortings, snifflings, nose blowings.

"Mr. McGee?" Joanna said. I turned toward them. They were under control, smiling, eyes slightly reddened. She dug

135

into her purse and took out a folded envelope and held it out to me. As I took it, she said, "This is a token of our appreciation for trying to help my sister and me, and Charles of course, and some small restitution for what you . . . had to endure at the hands of a man we once loved and trusted."

"You don't have to do this."

"I want to. It's out of my own funds. They say we won't be able to touch anything of Charles's for quite a long time, until it is all straightened out. I talked this over with my attorney, and he suggested that for tax purposes we both consider it as a gift. I will send you the same amount next year, and the same amount the year after. He said it would be better for both of us that way."

"I feel a little strange about this."

"For God's sake, why should you?" Terry said rudely. "If it wasn't for you, Charlie, bless him, would be dead. This broad is loaded and she's grateful. And you are permanently unemployed, by choice, aren't you, McGee? What's with this hesitation? You seem to be rejecting all kinds of little gifts lately." She winked broadly at me.

I put the envelope in my pocket. Nobody had been able to find the stuff they had checked out of my hotel. So I was wearing gift clothing. Gift from Nina. I had given her the measurements—44 extra-long, 35 waist, 35 inseam, shoes 13 C, shirts 17-35—and she had scurried around harassing people to cuff the pants, and had even bought one of Abercrombie's better suitcases to put the gear in. She bought far more than I had wanted, but aside from slightly hairier fabrics than I would have chosen, everything was fine.

Joanna put her hand in mine. Her eyes were shiny. She said goodby and went down to join her jolly, happy, uncomplicated husband.

"If he wants to keep busy," I said to Terry, "he can always run for office."

"Oh, you are very very funny. When is the little designer coming after you?"

"Her name is Nina. Three o'clock. What are you going to do?"

"Today, or from now on? Today I am going to go out and buy, buy, buy. Gaudy, expensive, ridiculous things. I am going to bully the clerks, make scenes, and buy, buy, buy. It's my therapy, darling. As to from now on, I shall get sister settled down, then go back to Athens, then down to Montevideo for Christmas with a flock of other professional house guests, then Mexico in the spring, and summer near Cannes, and

136

from then on plans are a bit vague. I expect I shall go right on being Terry Drummond."

There was a touching look of vulnerability about her.

"Good luck to Terry Drummond," I said.

"Sweetie, if you try to feel sorry for me, I shall hit you flush in the mouth."

I took the envelope out and opened it and looked at the figure on the check. It was a ridiculous figure. It was unreal. I tucked it away, resisting the temptation to take it out for another look to see if I could have misread it.

After our baggage was checked aboard, and while we waited for the flight to be announced, I told Nina about the envelope at the hotel. I had gone there on the off chance, and found they still had it. I had to sign an affadavit about the loss of the receipt, and then tell them exactly what was in it, so they could check the contents—with my approval.

"It belongs to you," I said.

"I keep hoping I can have a lot of time with him before they operate, Trav."

"It's more cash than I usually carry around, honey."

"Do you think Mike is scared of the operation?"

He wasn't scared. The time we spent there was strange. We had a rental car and two rooms in a motel about six miles from the hospital. In the morning we would have breakfast in the motel restaurant and then I would drive her to the hospital. We would both spend a little time with Mike, and then I would leave her there. It was cold gray November weather, with low clouds and a frequent misty rain. I had the days to myself. I had my own devils to wrestle. I worked at getting myself back into shape. When I forced exercises to the limit of endurance, I would think of the circus-girl look of Doris Wrightson and wonder what they were doing with her, and how they had managed to keep that sensation out of the public press.

At four-thirty I would go back and sit and talk with them for a half-hour and then take Nina back to the motel. We did not talk much. She seemed remote. We were not lovers. I had kissed her, but sensed a flavor of remoteness in her acceptance. She was too focused on her brother and, perhaps, on those evaluations of herself which came from all their talk. He was the only blood-closeness she had left.

Nightmares awoke me. In sleep, the things would come

137

out of the walls again. The worst ones were the shiny ones which rattled.

She had those three days with him, and at the end of the third day, before they began to prep him for the operation scheduled for the following morning, after she had kissed him and wished him luck, he asked me to stay a moment. "Man-talk," he told her.

"She's gone?"

"She's gone, Mike."

There was a smile on his ruined gaunted face. "Kid sister. We had to break through that. We had to find each other as people. I'm glad there was time for that."

"So is she."

"Big brother. Shattered hero. She had to look behind all that and find out who I am. Without the deification impulse. Just a guy. Now we like each other for the right reasons, Trav."

"These Gibsons are good folks."

"You're uneasy. You think I'm going to saddle you with kid sister forever. We talked about you two."

"Mike, I swear, the way it happened between us wasn't . . ."

"Don't insult me with that crap, Sergeant. She's a woman. She's capable of making choices. And neither of you are very effete or bloodless. It got her over that Plummer thing. And over the bitterness. She's in love with you."

"Are you sure of that?"

"More sure than she is. She's suspicious of it. She thinks it might be physical infatuation. But now that I know her, I don't think she could be a purely physical person in any relationship. There would have to be more, or it wouldn't work for her. But she knows, just as I know, that it would be a very foolish business to try to permanently halter McGee. You are too much of a maverick, Sergeant. Too roving and restless. Maybe a little too self-involved."

"I could be getting over that, Mike."

"Are you volunteering to marry my sister, you cad?"

"What the hell, Mike?"

"Don't get jumpy, boy. I asked you to stay behind so I could make certain that out of a lot of vague guilts, if I don't make it through this cutting session, you two idiots won't make a sentimental and emotional gesture and get yourselves stuck with each other. Marriage makes a lousy memorial. Pack her along with you, with my blessing, boy, and use her well. Otherwise the two of you will be walking around with steam coming out of your ears. Six months from now, if it all still percolates, then make a decision independent of guilt or memorials to me. If it is yes, I shall stare down in disbelief from Valhalla."

"Twenty years from now, you silly bastard, we will probably be running here to get some advice from you about your teen-age nephews and nieces. Bad advice."

He held his hand out toward me. I took it.

"McGee, deserve the girl. And afterwards, be someone for her to run to when she gets bruised. And when she does want to get married, you be my eyes—you take a good long searching look at the son of a bitch, and pry her loose if he can't cut it."

They kept him under the knife for six hours, and sent him back alive. Barely. He lasted for two days, and had a few moments of drugged consciousness, and when he went there was a gloom around that great big place that you could feel. They said the words and put him in the ground, and I took the pale and hollow-eyed and silent girl down to Lauderdale, to Slip F-18, Bahia Mar, and installed her aboard the Busted Flush, my fifty-two foot barge-type houseboat, diesel powered, offensively luxurious in all the right areas, and reasonably shipshape topsides. A frantic phone call had barely kept it from being sold out from under me. I gorged a frail bank account with Joanna's check. I introduced Nina around to the permanent characters, the Alabama Tiger and Captain Johnny Dow and all the rest of them. She made a good impression. I set her to work keeping house(boat) and as a deck hand. I browned her on the beach, and told her gaudy lies and stories to make her smile, and kept her so active and busy that her slight office softness was trimmed down to firm and lovely flesh. But all I could do was admire it. She had her own stateroom. She was not morose. She was not brooding. She was just very quiet and thoughtful, a little time of the deadness of the spirit. Sometimes there was an awkwardness between us when something accidental, some physical contact, would remind us that we were, quietly and deliberately, restricting our relationship to a casual basis.

I couldn't seem to throw off the nightmares. I felt very edgy at times. The Busted Flush never got so much earnest and dedicated maintenance. And I kept worrying about Christmas. It was coming along soon and I knew it would be rough for her.

She was the one who found the small item in the back of the *Miami News*. Mr. Baynard Mulligan had been given three years for embezzlement and tax evasion. He was appealing. The prosecution's case had been weakened when Mr. Mulligan had married one of the key witnesses against him, a Bonita Hersch, the secretary who had aided him in his raid on the Armister fortune, and who had been instrumental in his apprehension. Another secretary, a Doris Wrightson, had given testimony very damaging to Mulligan.

With the first genuine glint of humor I had seen in a long time, Nina said, "I'll bet he'll end up wishing he'd settled for twenty years."

I studied her. We were in stasis. We both needed to be jolted out of this strange drabness of spirit which was spoiling the game.

I said, "Let's cruise this thing down to the Keys, honey."

She looked startled. "Do you know how to run it, all alone?"

"I'll have you to help."

"That's pretty scary. I don't know anything about ropes and compasses and things."

"We'll blunder along."

I really think it was a fish who brought my love back to me—a fleet, six-pound, goggle-eyed bonefish. Cool wind and weather had cleared away the bugs. We went chugging down Florida Bay. Once she stopped being apprehensive, she became almost nonchalant at taking her trick at the wheel, reading the charts, spotting the markers. And one misty morning partway down, she discovered fish. She had never fished in her life. She was using one of my spinning outfits. The hard wrench at the line electrified her. It was a new world. She became a very intent, a very beady-eyed, a very dedicated fisherman. She lost some good ones and chewed herself out, and never made the same mistake more than twice. This was the first real sparkle of interest I had seen since Mike had died.

We went down into the Content Keys and found a sheltered cove and established residence. When we needed anything, we would take the dinghy and wind up the little limey outboard and chug on in to Ramrod. It was a quiet Christmas. I gave her a spinning outfit of her own, with a little pink plastic tackle-box and a gaudy array of lures. She was enchanted. She gave me two bottles of excellent brandy, a superior yachtsman's hat, and a little transistor radio to replace the one she had managed to drop over the side. Merry Christmas. Merry Platonic Christmas to all.

On a reasonably warm January afternoon, after we had taken a swim, she took the dinghy out alone to fish the flats. I was having a bad day. I stayed aboard. I had awakened exhausted by nightmares, listless, and without appetite. I tried to get some sun while she was fishing, but ended up pacing my top deck, wondering if the emotional damage which made me so edgy was permanent. Then I heard her whooping. She was standing up in the dinghy. There was some great commotion going on out there. I ran and got the glasses and put them on her. She was keeping the rod tip high, and as she circled toward me I could see that her face was practically bulging with intensity, determination and excitement. At about the moment I realized she had a reasonably good bonefish on, she lost her balance and fell out of the dinghy without foundering it. But she didn't drop the rod. She scrambled up. The water came just below her waist. She turned a grinning face toward the Busted Flush and whooped again. I watched her work him, and get him close, and move cautiously to the dinghy, make about four false tries, and then swoop up that gleaming silver length with the landing net. She piled aboard, did some bailing, and then came chugging home. I made the dinghy fast and then helped her over the rail. Her little blue sunsuit was sodden.

"Hey, isn't he glorious! Isn't he the damnedest thing? He went a thousand miles an hour! Around and around and around. What is he? Can we eat him?"

"He's a bonefish, and he's a nice one, and it is early for them around here. We can't eat him."

"No?"

"No."

She bit her lip, dropped to her knees, and worked him out of the net. His gills were working. She grasped him around the middle, lowered him and carefully dropped him into the water. He floated on his side, tail making weak movements. "Hurry along," she told him. "Go on about your business, Bonefish. You are a nifty fish. Go warn your relatives there's a girl around here named Gibson who's going to raise hell with your whole clan." He slowly righted himself, and gave a more powerful flicker of that tail, and went angling slowly down and away. "Come back yourself, any time," she called.

And she spun, joyous, grabbed me with round tan arms and fishy hands, pasted wet sunsuit against me, gave me a happy noisy kiss.

"Congratulations," I said, and kissed her in return.

She looked at me speculatively. The next kiss was longer. Her face changed and softened. "Bit on a little white dude," she said dreamily.

"Little crabs are better."

The next kiss was imperative. I swung her up and took her below. It was all back for us, more than before—a deeper, richer and more demanding hunger.

February, March, and into the loveliness of April.

Sometimes we moved to other coves, other beaches. Always private. We had no need for anyone else. She could sleep in my arms and sense the looming presence of nightmare and waken me, quiet me, soothe me. And little by little they went away. There was laughter aboard. And a vastly diminished laundry problem. Clothes were for when you got cold, or thought you heard a boat coming, or when you had to go ashore. There were a thousand permutations and combinations of love. By day and by night, very quick and very lengthy, comical and saddened, bawdy and spiritual, simple and complicated, mild and stormy. It seemed that we could never wear away that hard enduring edge of need, that the pace would never slacken.

But at last of course it did. A little less compulsive magic, but more of something else. The product of love and of the ten million words of history and revelation we spoke to each other. One day there was the unspoken awareness that we had to get back to the world. On a trip to Key West she had purchased, almost apologetically, tools of her trade. She began to do a little more drawing each day. And her lust for bonefish dwindled.

We sat topside one evening, holding hands, watching a vast fiery sunset. She was silent for a long time.

"Trav?"

"Yes, darling."

"I don't want you to think . . . I mean, I don't want to seem like . . ."

"Hush," I told her, and raised that small and valuable hand to my lips, kissed her fingertips and palm. "We'll take our time getting back to Lauderdale. How about five days?"

"How did you know?"

"The same way you knew it was time."

"And two days there, and then put me on a plane, darling. And don't let me look back, because if you do I won't be able to leave you. You knew I would?"

"When you were ready. Yes."

"I'll always love you. Can you understand that?"

"Yes, but don't ever try to make anyone else understand it, Nina."

"It will always be too private to tell."

And so it was an April magic, going back. Hauntingly sweet, because we knew this was the end of it. There was nostalgia in each caress.

Perhaps those weeks of us were, in one sense, a memorial. People have built imposing structures out of far meaner materials. I cherished her and celebrated her, and we restored each other.

SUSPENSE...
ADVENTURE...
MYSTERY...

John D. MacDonald's
TRAVIS McGEE SERIES

12